# SEARCHING FOR SULLIVAN

Carissa Ann Lynch

# SEARCHING FOR SULLIVAN

 LIMITLESS
PUBLISHING

Limitless Publishing, LLC
Kailua, HI 96734
www.limitlesspublishing.com

Formatting: Limitless Publishing

ISBN-13: 978-1-68058-954-2
ISBN-10: 1-68058-954-7

# DEDICATION

To all of my friends in dark places.

# CHAPTER ONE

My son inherited his name from my great-great granddad, Sullivan von Derbach. It is a respectable and stalwart family name; but in truth, I have never once called him by it. He has always been, and always will be, Sully to me.

When it comes to Sully, it is not the trips to Disney World, or other big events, that I remember most. It is the simplest of moments that cling to my soul and release their vengeful talons into the very heart of me. Like the first time Sully saw a shooting star. We were sitting in a clumsy pair of lawn chairs, staring up at the velvety pool of blackness, when a quick flash of light sprung down from the sky. He was only three at the time, and he screamed with such delight that the moment overwhelmed him, and he burst into tears of joy.

Or the time we baked one of those cheap, store-bought cakes. I absentmindedly laid the glass pan down on a forgotten burner, and the next thing I knew blue, pasty cake and glass shards exploded onto the ceiling and walls. Initially, we were

1

terrified. But then there we were: rolling in a fit of giggles on our backs as our eyes traveled the circumference of the room, examining the damages caused by our "cake bomb," as Sully called it.

When I wake up in the mornings, I focus every ounce of energy into concentrating on *those* memories, the good ones, before I get out of bed. But no matter how hard I try, my mind always drifts to the one memory that I cannot let go of—the summer Sully turned thirteen…

*We visited an old campsite at Lake Merlott that summer. It was the first time we'd been camping in seven years. I used to take him all the time when he was little, but as he grew older and my own workload and school schedule became more hectic, family activities, like camping, took a back burner.*

*The campsite was a regular lot that my father and his new wife, Judy, frequented on most holidays and weekends in the warmer months of the year. Judy and my father had been begging us to come up to "the camp" with them for years, and when I suggested it to Sully, I was nearly one hundred percent certain that his thirteen-year-old self would scoff at the idea. Instead, he surprised me by responding enthusiastically, "Sure. Let's do it, Mom."*

*Around the age of ten, Sully started becoming more temperamental and reclusive. The honest truth is that I was working and attending courses at the university, and his biological father had never been in the picture, so he was left to himself a lot of the time. He always seemed wise beyond his years, even*

2

*as a toddler, and we were always close, so I never worried too much about him. That is, until he became quieter, more distant.*

*As our camping trip approached, my concerns about Sully were becoming more and more worrisome. He'd recently acquired a girlfriend, and most of our interactions consisted of hostile remarks or non-responses—which were inherently worse. His body language said it all—he no longer liked his mother.*

*So, when I suggested the camping trip and he reacted so well, I felt relieved about the state of our relationship, and I was hyped up for the trip. Two days before we were scheduled to leave, I was taking a shortcut home from work when I saw the outdated RV sitting on the lawn of a well-kept Cape Cod-styled home. Impulsively, I yanked the car over to the side of the road, barely missing the curb.*

*The cardboard "For Sale" sign that leaned on its bumper was weather-faded and difficult to read, but I could see that the asking price was $1600. It was too much for my budget, but considering the age of the sign, I was hoping for a motivated seller. I knocked on the door, my checkbook in hand, channeling the most confident version of myself. The bald, pot-bellied man that answered the door with a grunt was not what I was hoping for. But when I offered the check for one thousand dollars, he smiled kindly and handed me the keys. "First, I have to make sure that it runs and that it's not a dump on the inside," I informed him sternly, pulling the check back away from his pudgy, grasping fingers.*

*He shrugged. "Let me get my shoes." He met me out in the yard beside the RV several minutes later.*

*The interior was not new or anywhere near perfect, but it surpassed my expectations. It seemed well taken care of, free of debris or any major damages on the inside. Most importantly, it seemed to be in working order. It took a few tries to get it started, but that didn't surprise me after hearing that it'd been sitting unused for nearly five years now. We sealed the deal with a handshake, and I signed the check.*

*Driving home that day, I can still recall the rush of excitement that I felt down deep in the pit of my belly. I had purchased plenty of vehicles before, but never anything like this, and never so spur of the moment. It was an "impulse buy," but I felt great about it.*

*I realized then that it was Sully's pleasant reaction to the idea of camping that drove me to stop when I saw it. I wanted this weekend to be perfect between us, and I viewed it as an opportune time for me to make up for my own busy schedule, and subsequent absence from his life. I needed some one-on-one time with my son; simple as that.*

*You can imagine my disappointment when his girlfriend showed up as we were loading our food and clothing into the camper on the morning we were scheduled to leave. I looked from her to Sully, my confusion and irritation transparent. "I invited her to go with us," Sully explained, shrugging his shoulders in a "no big deal" sort of way that he recently had a habit of doing. Some of his mannerisms had begun to drive me insane.*

*"Your parents okay with this?" I asked her, raising my eyebrows at the girl skeptically. She nodded, focusing her attention on a wad of gum that was stuck to the sole of a bright, orange Nike high top.*

*"My parents said it was fine. They aren't even home on the weekends usually, anyway. They're probably glad I'm with another adult instead of home on my own," she replied sulkily. I couldn't help but wonder what kind of parents would leave their kid home alone on the weekends, and I definitely couldn't fathom why any sane parent would allow their barely-a-teen daughter to go camping overnight with a strange boy, parents or no parents.*

*Perhaps I was being sexist, but I know that if Sully had been a girl, I would have kept a tighter leash on him than I did. I guess my parenting was no better than theirs though, because I said "okay" and allowed my son to bring this young girl camping with us despite my better judgment.*

*When I pictured this camping adventure in my mind's eye, I imagined driving with Sully next to me in the passenger seat of the front cab, shooting the shit and enjoying the open road. A supreme bonding experience. But instead, he and "Roxy"—that's what she called herself, but I suspected it wasn't her real name—were seated on a couch in the back, talking cheerily amongst themselves in hushed tones. Whenever I stole a glance at them in the rearview mirror, they responded with looks of disgust.*

*It was a strange feeling, watching this son of*

*mine talking so easily and freely to Roxy, while every conversation between us for the past two years had been awkward and strained. I couldn't help but feel a twinge of jealousy. I wanted my son back.*

*Four long hours later, we arrived at "the camp" at Lake Merlott. We were greeted by my father, Ralph, his wife, Judy, my sister, Margaret, and her new baby girl, Maxie. We spent our first night at camp pretty typically; we sat around the bonfire, chatting while roasting marshmallows and hotdogs on wooden sticks. Most of the conversation revolved around eighteen-month-old Maxie. She was quite a little ham, running around playing peek-a-boo and smiling up at each of us to reveal a semi-toothless grin. She was such a doll, and she was my first niece, so I was glad to spend time with her, as well as the rest of my family.*

*Sully and Roxy joined us around the campfire, but they kept their fold-up chairs slightly farther back from ours, and they whispered quietly amongst themselves. I couldn't help but wonder how these two young children could have so much to talk about. Again with the jealousy, I suppose.*

*We all decided to turn in early, heading to our separate RVs, with plans to go boating on my father and Judy's newest addition in the morning: a twenty-three foot Caravelle Interceptor, which was basically a really fast speedboat. I'm not a big fan of swimming or watersports, but Sully seemed interested in going, and I was eager to appease him and my father.*

*Our camper consisted of three beds—a queen-*

*sized bed in the back for me, a twin-sized sleeper bed that folded out from the dining table, and a large sleeping space above the cab section in front. I may have been cool for allowing Roxy to join us on this excursion, but I would not let them sleep in the same bed. That is where I drew the line.*

*"You there, and you there," I told them, pointing first to the upper bed for Sully, and the table fold-out bed for Roxy. Luckily, they were too tired to argue with me, and they climbed into their respective beds. We were all asleep within minutes. There's just something about sleeping in the middle of nowhere that brings on the best quality of sleep.*

*I woke up early the next day with the soft, wavering glow of the morning sun peeking through the moth-eaten, flimsy curtains that covered the tiny windows on both sides of my bed. I nudged Sully and Roxy awake. "We're going out on Grandpa's Interceptor today," I told Sully, trying to give him sufficient motivation to get out of bed. He had never been much of a morning person, and getting him up for school over the years had basically been hell. My own mother had this incredible ability to wake me up with a cheery voice and a smile every morning as a child. Regrettably, I did not inherit said trait.*

*But Sully surprised me by getting right up that morning, as did his girlfriend. We took turns changing into our bathing suits and shorts in the cramped toilet space next to my bed, and after a quick breakfast, and the lengthy process of loading up towels, coolers, and life jackets into the boat, we headed out for the half mile drive to Lake Merlott.*

*My father drove the truck with Judy in the passenger seat, while the rest of us rode in the boat, which was securely hitched to the truck. My sister sat beside me in the back bench seat, bouncing baby Maxie up and down, up and down, on her knees to keep her satisfied. Sully and Roxy took their seats as far away from me as possible, up in the front bow of the boat.*

*There were nearly sixty camping lots at Lake Merlott and as we rode past all of them, the breeze blew generously, providing relief from the scorching heat of the sun. It was apparently not a huge camping weekend because most of the lots were vacant. A few of them contained RVs or tents, and I offered a friendly wave to the families we passed.*

*For an instant, I was overcome with a rush of my own childhood memories of coming to Lake Merlott, and riding just like this in the back of one of my father's boats. I imagined my own thirteen-year-old self sticking my arm out the side of the boat, making waving motions with my hand, all the while giggling excitedly with my mousy brown hair blowing all around my face and sticking to the corners of my mouth. When my mother was alive, she never rode in the truck with dad. She was always in the back, seated right between me and my sister. I missed my mother terribly, and as I looked at Sully, I was reminded that life was too short, and I must continue to do everything within my power to gain a closer relationship with my only son before it was too late.*

*Even though he was a boy, he looked so much*

8

*like me at his age. I imagined him with longer hair
and girlish eyes—he was the spitting image of me.
That realization made me proud. "Cheer up," my
sister, Margaret, said, nudging me playfully. Maxie
suddenly reached her small pudgy arms out to me,
and I took her willingly onto my lap. I planned on
enjoying this day, smiling down into my baby
niece's sparkling green eyes. She smiled back
toothily, and I felt utter calmness and peace.*

*We followed a tree-lined, rutty road that
eventually opened up to reveal the sixty acre spread
of freshwater that made up Lake Merlott. The
weather was perfect for a day on the boat. When I
looked over at Sully, he was staring right at me, and
we smiled at one another—a real smile—for the
first time in nearly a year. I wished I could seize the
perfectness of that moment. If only my eyelids were
like shutters on a camera, and I could capture it all
as I blinked...if only.*

*Even though it was the height of boating season,
the ramp was unexpectedly deserted, much like the
campsite itself. At the water's edge, my father exited
the truck and boarded the boat. Judy backed the
truck up expertly as my father guided it off the
trailer. My mother never was much of a driver, and
I was impressed to see Judy handling the process
with ease.*

*My father assumed his position behind the wheel
of the boat and circled around the shallow waters,
waiting to pick up Judy at the dock. Moments later,
she was standing on the edge of the wooden, rickety
boat dock, waving with a gleeful expression on her
face. I liked Judy; always had. She might not have*

been my mother, but she was a good woman and she loved my father, which was all that really mattered.

After my mom died, it took five years for my father to find Judy. Five years might not seem very long to most people, but I was relieved when he finally met someone. My mother was the type of woman who laid out my father's underwear and socks in the morning. My father needed a woman to take care of him—I'm glad that woman was Judy.

Sully and Roxy's first request was to ride on the donut-shaped tube that was attached to the back of the boat. Margaret had one of those disposable cameras that you buy at the Quickmart, and she handed it to me gaily. We rode in companionable silence, snapping photos of Sully and Roxy as they cackled excitedly and held onto the float for dear life.

After tubing, there was swimming and a break for slapping together sandwiches and pulling out chip bags. Everything tastes better on a boat; I'm not sure why, but I swear it's true. By the time we finished eating, it was late afternoon, and the sun had shifted lazily behind a fluffy bed of clouds.

Although most of us were more than ready to head back to camp, Sully insisted on doing a little fishing first. He had my dad doing circles around the lake in search of the perfect spot. He finally settled on a fairly shallow, secluded spot that was barely ten feet from a shore bank. The shore was lined with thick, gnarly roots, ancient oak trees, and overgrown shrubbery.

It was only five minutes after casting his line that

*the raindrops started to fall. "Time to head back. We don't want to get caught in a storm," I warned him.*

*Lucky for us, the back of the boat was sheltered by a medium-sized canopy. I held baby Maxie on my lap under it, using my hands to shield her from any excess rainwater that might drip into her eyes.*

*Judy, Roxy, and Margaret squeezed in beside me but Sully, being his usual macho and stubborn self, remained in the front bow of the boat, gripping his fishing pole with a tense expression.*

*I was tempted to warn him that he would catch cold, sitting out there in the rain, but I hesitated, not wanting to sound too motherly in front of his girlfriend. Instead I gave him a stern look, and he reeled in his line begrudgingly.*

*Dad had never budged from his position behind the wheel, and he turned the key to fire up the engine on the boat. Nothing happened.*

*An angry slew of curse words poured out of my father's mouth, and we all sat there in stony silence, not wanting to agitate him further. I swear I think we were all holding our breaths for a moment there.*

*Again and again he tried to get the engine to turn over, but there was still nothing but the sound of the rain, and thunder roared in the distance.*

*Why were we not smart enough to check a weather report? The abandoned boat docks and vacant camping lots should have been a clue for us...*

*"Did you run it out of gas, honey?" Judy finally asked, in a whiny, mildly irritated tone. My father shot her a look that left no room for a verbal*

11

*response. My father wasn't that stupid. I knew we weren't out of gas.*

*He continued to crank the engine. I don't know much about boats, but I know that if you keep on cranking, you will eventually kill the battery.*

*"Dad, do you have your cell phone handy? Maybe we should call for help..." I began to suggest, but then the boat came to life, and the beautiful roar of the speedboat's engine was tremendously comforting. I let out a sigh of relief and adjusted baby Maxie on my lap.*

*As we began our lengthy journey back to the boat dock, we were in the throes of the storm. The once sunny sky was now shrouded in darkness, making it impossible to discern the time of day. Lightning struck in the distance, and angry torrents of waves swept high along the sides of the boat, knocking us around unsteadily and beating our faces with pricks of water pellets.*

*I was still holding the baby, and I squeezed her tight, pushing out images of her bouncing off of my lap and into the fierceness of the stormy waters.*

*I thought our biggest concern was being stranded in Lake Merlott, but riding through this storm was proving to be quite an ominous task. The rain came down in sheets now, the water so rough that Dad slowed down to a speed just slightly above drifting. The wind was picking up in speed and strength too.*

*I worried that the entire canopy might be yanked off its poles; or worse, collapse on top of all of us.*

*My worries were instantly replaced with a new fear as I caught a glimpse of the size and roughness of the waves up ahead. We hadn't even seen the worst of it yet...*

*I gripped Maxie and I braced myself for the impact. As we hit the first wave with a slam, I held tight to the baby, probably hard enough to bruise her tiny arms.*

*A shrill, panicky scream came out of the baby's mouth, and the sound of it was alarming. The next slam jarred my entire body. My butt came off the seat, and I clenched my teeth so tightly, they ached painfully.*

*Then the boat jerked to the right so hard, it threatened to tip on its side. Water came up over the sides and we continued to endure slam after slam, wrestling with the treacherous waves.*

*Sounds of shouting echoed in my ears...but this time, I recognized the cries as my own.*

*How did this storm hit so quickly and violently, without any warning signs?*

*A mixture of rain and lake water drenched my face, and I held an arm up in front of Maxie protectively, shielding her from the water as much as I could.*

*The rain was pouring down in a blinding rage, making it impossible to see what lie ahead.*

*After what seemed like hours, but was probably seconds, the boat stopped rocking, and I was able to catch my breath again.*

*I reached over to clasp my sister's hand in mine. "She's okay," I assured her, talking about baby Maxie, who I still held tightly in my arms. Margaret's face was white as a sheet. She's in shock, I realized, trying to catch her eye and offer some assurances.*

*But then she pointed slowly toward the front of the boat, to the bow where Sully was sitting. Or was supposed to be sitting, I should say. Sully was gone.*

*That* moment—when my eyes landed on his empty seat—is the most persistent memory of them all. It is *the* moment when my entire life changed.

It is the dividing line that split my life into two separate halves—the part where I had a son, and then the part where I never saw him again.

It is this second part that I find myself stuck, forever entwined in its murky, unforgiving waters. *Those* waters—more dangerous than the ones in the throes of a storm—hold me hostage, never letting me forget that once upon a time I lived another life—a life that contained my heart, my son...

# CHAPTER TWO

That was five years ago. Try as I might to blot out the events of that day, the memories invade my psyche and overrun my thoughts on a daily basis. I nearly drowned myself that day, jumping into the stormy waters and probing the murky, sightless lake until my lungs nearly exploded inside my own chest.

The sheriff who eventually pulled me out of the water was named Billy Joe Baggins. Sheriff Baggins and his deputies called in a dive team from a neighboring county, and they searched the lake countless times over the course of four weeks. Sully was a good swimmer. But the facts were there. And I have *always*, unfortunately, been a stickler for the facts.

The fact was that they found blood on the side of the boat, and deducted that he hit his head during the brutal storm as he was slammed around in the front of the boat. I know how rough of a ride it was—I was there.

I was so worried about my damn niece that day

15

that I never really thought about what could happen to my teenage son. Looking back on it now, I don't know what I was thinking. I should have been up there in the front, protecting him from the storm.

He was probably unconscious when he hit the water, causing his body to sink to the bottom like a rock, at least that's how they described it to me.

Lake Merlott empties out into the Meade River, making it likely that my son's body floated downstream and ended up God knows where.

This is the part when I should declare that I know he's still alive and he must be out there somewhere, but that is not the case. I would love nothing more than to find my son, but I know in my heart he is dead.

The tombstone that marks his empty grave is located in Flocksdale Cemetery, which is where my mother is buried. Like her, he died too young.

People always wonder how I dealt with the pain of his loss, and I understand this curiosity wholeheartedly because once upon a time, I wondered the same thing about parents who lost young children. The honest answer is that you just do. You *just do*.

You take one day at a time and you just keep living. Or there's the alternative—giving up. I may be many things—some of them bad—but I'll never be a quitter.

\*\*\*

When I became a parent, all of my concern for myself shifted to my child. I no longer lived for me,

16

but for him. Now that he is gone, a strange thing has happened. I've reverted back to this world of it being just me. So, here it is—just me, in my own little "me bubble."

My name is Veronica von Derbach. I have a PhD in psychology. I live in a small garden apartment in Crimson County, but I am rarely home. Number of children—*zero*.

My main focus in life at this point is my career as a psychologist.

I used to love diagnostics and testing—the technical side of things—but that all changed when Sully died.

I've recently developed an unusual interest in a controversial branch of psychology called parapsychology, which is the psychological study of paranormal events. In other words, I study ghosts.

Experts in the field of psychology, in general, look down their noses at my area of expertise.

The only person in my own professional circle who respects my interests is my supervisor, mentor, and closest thing to a friend, Dr. Pollyanna Paddison. We have known each other since we were undergrads.

It was the first day of spring semester, and I had a meeting with her.

Her office was cramped and stuffy, but it did have a window in it and was secluded from everyone else's office, which was more than I can say for my own office.

My office is set in the center of the main hallway on the first floor, so I have to deal with a lot of student traffic and everyday questions such as,

"Where is my statistics class?" or better yet, "Where is the ladies' room?" I could just close my door to the noise and distractions, but that would contradict my acclaimed "open-door policy" that I tried to adhere to while teaching during fall semester.

Dr. Paddison was sitting in a high-backed, swivel chair behind an antique maple desk. Every time I come up here, I can't help but wonder how in the world anyone hauled that heavy, old desk up three flights of stairs, when I know it couldn't fit in the elevator with its mammoth-like size.

She was scribbling on a notepad with her head tucked down in thought, but I knew she could sense my presence.

"Come on in, Veronica." She waved her hand without a glance upward in my direction.

I took a seat on the other side of her desk, unfolding a U.S. map on my lap. Then I got my pen, handheld notebook, and sticky tabs ready.

Dr. Paddison flipped her own notebook over, looking satisfied with herself. She leaned down and picked up a stack of something from the floor behind her desk, then she sat a stack of slim, manila folders on the desk in front of her.

Her desk and office floor were covered with dusty books, random student papers, and office supplies. I had no idea how she kept track of anything in here, but it seemed to work for her because she was a brilliant teacher.

"Are you ready to hit the road again?" she asked, raising her eyebrows at me and smiling. She already knew the answer. I hate being stuck in one place. At least I hate it now; I didn't used to, when I was a mother.

"As ready as I can be." I impatiently adjusted my notebook and map.

"Okay, then. Let's get started, shall we?" Opening the top file folder, she licked her finger like an old school marm, flipping through sheets of paper that I couldn't read from where I was sitting.

At the end of this powwow, she was going to give me the files anyway, to peruse through on my own. I wished she would just hand them over and let me review them on my own time, but I had a great deal of respect for Dr. Paddison, so I just let her do her thing.

"I've been flooded with so many requests and reports, and I've tried to prioritize and pick the cases most suitable for your expertise…

I'm going to give you three cases to start with, and then you can call me from the road like last time, and I'll assign you more at that time. I'm still trying to sort through some of them…" She moved more papers around on her desk, exasperated.

I felt sorry for her. Dr. Paddison not only manages these said reports, but she also teaches three classes of her own and manages me and the other seven faculty members in the Psychology department. I also know she has two small children at home, which makes me sympathize with her even more. Needless to say, she is a busy lady…

"Make sure you bring your fax machine with you so I can send more case files while you're on the road," she mumbled, still looking around her desk for something.

"Case number one. The subject's name is Bartholomew Eckleby. He's a seventy-one-year-old farmer from Pierce, Nebraska. He lives on a forty-two acre farm. Recently widowed. He lost his wife after a six-year battle with cancer, specifically lymphoma. I don't think they had any children. He's been calling incessantly. He swears his dead wife has been visiting him, moving objects around the house, and according to him, she recently returned home to claim her favorite ring. He's also convinced she's been roaming the woods behind his old farmhouse, wearing the white gown that she wore on the day of their wedding. He's considering paying a small fortune to have her body exhumed, but he's looking for help from us before he goes down that avenue."

I nodded, staying silent as I scribbled notes furiously into my notebook. When I was done, I placed a thin strip of sticky tab on the state of Nebraska.

"Case two?" I asked, glancing up at her momentarily.

"The second case comes from Cheyenne, Wyoming. Family of four. Mother and father are supposedly happily married. They have two children, a fourteen-year-old boy and a six-year-old girl. The young girl has been waking up nightly, screaming with night terrors. She swears that a demon is terrorizing her at night. Her parents chalked it all up to bad dreams at first, but the girl has bruises and claw marks to prove it. She has even drawn a disturbing picture of the demon." Dr. Paddison held up a pencil drawn sketch of a scary looking black blob with pointy teeth and claws for hands. I glanced at it, then bent my head to take more notes.

"The family is traumatized and considering hospitalization for the girl..." Dr. Paddison closed one file and opened another.

"Case three comes as a request from the mayor's office in Lansing, Michigan. He wants to keep this whole thing hush-hush, but he's heard of your good reputation and has requested you specifically."

I stopped writing and looked up at her, my expression worrisome.

I didn't typically handle high profile cases. Correction: I've *never ever* handled a high profile case before. This could either make me or break me in terms of my reputation, and I wasn't crazy about assuming that type of risk. Despite my concerns, I nodded, bowed my head, and kept writing.

"Mayor Fish is also married with two children. Two teenage boys. The entire family is reporting paranormal experiences. Chairs levitating, plates shattering, terrifying sounds, etcetera. Sounds like a possible poltergeist," she said hesitantly.

She closed the third file and handed me all three of them. I slid them inside my briefcase and folded up my map.

"I know the Mayor's case is important because of who he is, but my closest destination is Nebraska, and then Wyoming. He can't get special treatment because of his status. I will see him third, if that's okay with you," I announced boldly.

"I would expect no less from you." She chuckled, standing up by pushing on her chair arms.

I stood up as well, picking up my briefcase.

"Call me if you have any questions or problems along the way," Dr. Paddison said, gripping my hand in hers.

"Absolutely," I promised.

# CHAPTER THREE

After that weekend at Lake Merlott, I think everyone expected me to sell or simply dispose of the RV. What they don't seem to understand is that the RV is the final place where my son laid his head, and it contains an array of memories for me, not all of which are unpleasant. Plus, having the RV for my travels has proven to be quite beneficial.

I spent the weekend vacuuming the camper's floors, and stocking its cramped cabinetry in the tiny kitchen space with non-perishable food items, paper plates and cups, cleaning supplies, and toiletries.

The two cabinets above my bed were reserved for clothing and personal items. I also had some closet space for my notebooks, tools of the trade, and spare towels.

The RV might be outdated, but when I started traveling for work, I let myself splurge on a few modern things. I invested in one of those sweet, single-cup Keurig coffee makers. I also added a few updates to the décor, which included new shag rugs

23

to cover the dingy, stained carpet beneath, and a good, thick set of drapes to ward off the sun's glare.

These days, I prefer the dark.

Most importantly, I invested in a GPS system. Without it, I don't think I could do this job. I wasn't the best when it came to map reading, and I rarely relied on those sites like MapQuest. According to my GPS, the small, farming town of Pierce, Nebraska was approximately twelve and a half hours from Crimson County.

With the RV packed and Sully's picture secured to the dash, I was ready to head out on the road. If I stayed on track with the GPS's directions, I would hopefully get to Bartholomew Eckleby's farm by sundown.

Whenever I haven't driven the RV in a while, I always think about Sully when I first get behind the wheel. I think back to that summer day when I was discontent because I had to sit up front by myself while he chatted with that girlfriend of his. It's funny how death puts everything into perspective. What I wouldn't give now just to catch a glimpse of him in the rearview mirror. Now I ride alone.

Despite the initial influx of memories, driving was typically therapeutic for me. Well, if you consider the mind numbing state of blankness that my brain reverts to while driving therapeutic...

\*\*\*

Pierce, Nebraska seemed smaller than I expected. With a population of less than two thousand, it was your quintessential small farming

24

town. The first thing I saw when I came into town was a fourteen acre arboretum filled with woody plants, shrubbery, and trees. The sun was slipping, the greenery glittering with a ghostly glow.

The trees opened up into grassy farmlands, and within twenty minutes, I'd reached Mr. Eckleby's farm.

I knew it was his precisely because there was a sign declaring it so. I followed a narrow dirt path that lay between two stone pillars and the rickety Eckleby sign at the front.

I immediately noticed that the land was well taken care of. And I couldn't help wondering how a man of his age managed all of this farmland on his own.

As I navigated the camper down the path, I saw a horse stable, cow house, and rabbit hutch to my left. In the distance were silhouettes of cattle grazing and a beautiful white mare that reminded me of a dream I had once.

To the right was a barn filled with tractor equipment that looked shiny and new, and in the middle of it all was an old farmhouse that looked like a picture from one of those homey magazines.

I pulled into a wide graveled space neatly lined with stones, then parked. Bartholomew Eckleby must have been waiting for me by the door because he was standing next to the RV before I could even shut down the engine and step out.

"Veronica von Derbach," I said, wiping the sweat from my palms and offering my hand. He hesitated for an instant, and then offered his hand in return.

"Thanks for coming. Come inside." He motioned toward the charming farmhouse behind him. Following him, I said, "Your home is beautiful, Mr. Eckleby. Do you have laborers to help with the farm work?" For his age, he seemed athletic and fit, with soft, black hair that contained only mere specks of gray. But still, a farm this big...certainly he had some help...

"I have several fellas that I pay to help me," he answered briskly. "And please call me Bart." He held open a solid white, vinyl screen door and waited for me to walk in ahead of him. We walked through a parlor into an enormous white kitchen. It was equipped with a giant, floor-to-ceiling brick fireplace that was unlike anything I'd ever seen in a kitchen. There appeared to be a dining room area off of that space, but the kitchen itself was so spacious that it had its own table, a sturdy oak heirloom with enough seating for twelve people.

Bart selected a chair at the head of the table, and because I didn't want to sit a mile away from him, I chose the next seat over. I couldn't imagine living in such a big old house all by myself. Its beauty seemed somewhat gloomy and depressing when I imagined eating TV dinners in the same seat every night alone, with all that empty space around me.

But I knew what it felt like to be surrounded by empty chairs, and it can make even small spaces gray, dull, and depressing...

Bart folded his hands together on the table in front of him. His hands were the one feature that revealed his age, with reddish brown age spots and paper thin skin covering his bony knuckles. He suddenly covered one hand with the other, as though he could read my thoughts.

"I know that you've already told your story to Dr. Paddison from the university, but please tell me again," I asked, using my teeth to remove the cap on a ballpoint pen. I quietly opened my notebook. He sighed.

"The first time that I saw her...Mattie, that is...she's my wife, or *was* my wife, I should say..." His hands and shoulders were trembling, and I resisted the urge to reach out and hug him. This strong, sturdy farmer suddenly seemed vulnerable and fragile, making my heart ache.

"Anyways, I lost Mattie to cancer two years ago. She meant the world to me. I know what you're thinking...you're one of those people who think they're a doctor and who thinks everybody is crazy...but I'm *not* crazy and I didn't imagine this in my mind! And I'm not trying to conjure up my wife's ghost simply because I miss her..."

I put up a hand to stop him. I resisted the urge to tell him that I am, in fact, a doctor. "Bart, I promise—I don't believe you're making this up or that you're crazy. I'm here because I want to help you get to the bottom of this. I'm *not* here to berate your reports or try to disprove them. I only want to help."

Although I meant what I said, it was partially a lie. Whenever I conduct this type of research, my number one goal is to seek out a logical and/or psychological cause of the event. My second goal is to try to recreate the event and observe, objectively, any results that I find. My last and final goal is to provide some sort of explanation to the family and try to help them, just as a therapist would during a counseling session.

Explaining this to him would probably make him angry. I really did want to help him, if only because I know what it feels like to lose the love of your life.

"Please go on with your story," I gently encouraged, setting down my pen so I could just listen and give him my full attention.

"About a month ago, I woke in the night. Couldn't sleep. I've always had problems staying asleep through the night. There's a porch in the back. Mattie never let me smoke in the house. Now that's she gone, I could just do it if I wanted to and there'd be no one to stop me…but I just keep up the tradition, and I take my breaks on the porch, just like Mattie would want me to. When I went out there that night, I saw something moving out in the trees. I know it was her. She was dressed in white, just like she was on our wedding day, and the day of her funeral too.

I could see her walking out there! And then the next night, I stayed up all night waiting for her, but nothing happened. The same thing the next night: nothing. But then a week later, it happened again. I saw her out there, a white angel floating through the trees. I tried to run toward her, calling her name, but then she was gone. Poof! Just like that. And then it happened again last night," he confided, in a voice barely above a whisper.

I nodded. "What other things have happened, Bart?" I asked, leaning forward and placing a hand over his. Something about this man reminded me of my own father, and that caused a twinge of pain in my chest just thinking about it. After Sully's death, I'd distanced myself from my father...everyone else, for that matter. I missed my dad terribly.

Bart was chewing on his bottom lip, considering my question. "What is it, Bart? You can tell me," I urged.

"After it happened the second time, I thought I heard her in the house, and then a few days later, I realized her favorite diamond ring was missing, and some of her other jewelry pieces were moved around."

"For argument's sake, is it possible that you could have just simply misplaced the ring?" I had to ask.

He shook his head firmly. "I placed her ring in her jewelry box right after she died. I've never moved it since that day. Sure, I've opened the lid a couple times to take a peek at it, but that's it. I did it because I miss her sometimes, you know...but I didn't move it." His voice was starting to crack a little.

"I'm sorry. I know losing her must have been difficult for you," I said. I was tempted to tell him about my own loss, but this wasn't about me or Sully, and I didn't want to take away from his own feelings for Mattie.

"Does someone clean your house regularly?" He shook his head again.

"Not regularly. I can manage the inside on my own. That's the least I can do, considering that I can't manage much of the physical labor no more."

He held his head down, as though he felt ashamed for using help.

"The Merry Maids came a few times when I needed a good, overall cleaning. But when they were in the house, I was too, so I know they didn't rob me," he explained solemnly. I nodded, thinking it over.

"Is there anything else I need to know?" I asked, fighting off a yawn from sheer exhaustion after driving for nearly thirteen hours.

"I think that's it. Do we want to do a stakeout tonight?" he asked, an eager tone to his voice.

"I'm sorry, Bart. I'm exhausted tonight. I like to do my investigations when I'm well-rested. I will begin first thing in the morning, I promise. Also, I would like to gather observations on my own, if it's okay with you. That way, I can focus on the task at hand, and be completely objective in my findings. I'll be asking you questions along the way as needed, and I will keep you informed on what I find. But in the meantime, I want you to carry on with your daily routine while I concentrate on figuring this out. Is that okay with you?" I asked, hoping that I didn't sound too hard or cruel.

"Fine by me," he said. "Would you like to stay in the house? I have plenty of space, as you can see." He held his hands up to indicate the entirety of this huge space.

"I like to stay in my own camper. But at some point, in the next day or so, I may opt to sleep inside if it benefits the investigation." Once again, I was trying not to sound ungrateful.

"Okay. But I do insist on one thing. You need to

take your meals inside with me. You may be surprised to learn that I've always done most of the cooking, even when Mattie was still alive. Cooking is my passion, and when I was young, I almost went to school to become a trained chef," he said, his face beaming with pride. My mouth fell open in surprise. I certainly hadn't expected this elderly farmer to be a whiz in the kitchen.

I'd planned to have macaroni and cheese or ramen for supper, which suddenly didn't sound so appealing. "I'm going to make my famous chicken Gorgonzola pasta and homemade garlic bread, if you'd care to join me." My mouth watered just thinking about it. How could I say no?

Apparently, Gorgonzola is a type of cheese. I honestly was clueless as to what it was until Bart held up a plastic mixing bowl filled with medium-sized, bluish-green chunks of cheese that smelled extraordinary. I'd seen people make their own pasta on TV, but I didn't think people actually did it in real life. At least, not anyone I knew. When I craved spaghetti or fettuccini, I simply made a trip to the supermarket and bought one of those one dollar boxes of dry noodles. I usually added a dollar jar of generic sauce to go with it.

I offered to help him, but he insisted on preparing it all by himself. I could tell by the way he glided through the kitchen effortlessly that he was in his element now. This man, who moments earlier had appeared sullen and aged, now floated around the kitchen with vibrancy and merriment.

He combined flour and salt on a pastry board. Then he whisked together eggs, milk, and olive oil, adding them into the center of the floury mixture. He pressed his knuckles into the dough, kneading it all together, and then he rolled it flat with a rolling pen.

I stood up and leaned against the kitchen island, watching him work with admiration. His wife was one lucky woman when she was alive. If there really was a way to visit loved ones from the grave, I could understand why Mattie would want to return home to her life with him. He was certainly a splendid host, and a whiz in the kitchen.

Bart sliced thin strips out of the dough, and it finally started to look like pasta. He sautéed strips of chicken breast in a skillet and he baked buttery garlic bread in the oven, all the while stirring the delicious smelling cheese sauce and pasta on the stove. The smells overpowered my senses, and my mouth literally watered as I waited. For the life of me, I couldn't remember the last thing I'd eaten. Regardless of what it was, this was definitely going to be better.

"May I set the table at least?" I pleaded.

"Sure." He pointed me in the direction of his silverware and dishes in the far left cupboards and drawers. I took my time setting out our dinner places. I found a narrow vase in one of the cabinets, so I filled it with water and went outside to look for a few dainty flowers to fill it with. The sun had set and the land was cloaked in darkness. There was dull, yellow light from a bulb on the front porch, and it illuminated a few feet of yard space and the front porch steps.

There were yellow daisies and a red rose bush,

but I wanted to use this opportunity to explore a bit.

I walked the perimeter of the old farmhouse until I rounded a corner to its backside. This was the back porch that Bart referred to in our earlier discussion, the place where he smoked his cigarettes. This thought was confirmed by a sun-faded Adirondack chair and an ashtray filled to the brim with stubbed out butts.

I looked out toward the wooded area in the distance. In the dark, I could make out the shapes of a thousand trees beyond the tree line, and behind them was a backdrop of fog-covered, rolling hills.

My eyes scanned the entirety of the tree line, and then I glanced up at the dinky porch light that hung by a string of electrical wire. Unlike the one on the front porch, this one was inoperable. Without light, I wondered how easy it would be to see a woman walking in the woods at night time. It was certainly something to think about.

I selected a few white daisies next to the back porch and I carried them back inside to the table. Bart was pouring two glasses of white wine, and adding a handful of pistachios to the cheese sauce.

"Can you tell me about your laborers? How many do you have?" I asked, sipping the wine as he poured the creamy sauce over a plateful of pasta. He added a crunchy slice of bread to my plate. "Well, I have four workers. Salazar and Sampson, the twins. And then an old rancher and friend of mine, Mitch. And then a Latina woman named Carmen."

I dug into the pasta. It was rich and creamy, with a nutty flavor and aroma. I'd never had anything quite like it. It was like heaven on a fork.

When I glanced up from my plate to look at my host, I realized he hadn't even taken a bite of his own yet. He was watching me scarf down the meal with a look of self-satisfaction. He was obviously pleased with himself.

"It's so good," I admitted, smiling at him sheepishly. I ate until my plate was clean, but I declined his offer for more. I decided that when I got back home, I was definitely going to start making my own pasta, at least on occasion. Bart's pasta put my two-dollar spaghetti dinner to shame.

"To answer your earlier question—the twins work Tuesdays, Thursdays, and Saturdays. Mitch and Carmen are here on the other days. They all get along fine and they give me no problems whatsoever. If they did, I'd have fired them by now. They milk the cows, tend to the horses and rabbits, and take care of the land. I have about ten rows of crops now. I used to have more but it's gotten to be too much with my age. Mitch is the one in charge of the vegetables, and he tends to all of the crops while he's here."

"What are their hours? I didn't see anyone when I got here today." I wiped my mouth with a white linen napkin.

"They work sun up to sun down. Today was the twins' day, and sometimes I let them leave early. They're young fellas, barely in their twenties. They're always eager to leave in the evenings. They like to tend to their social lives, and all that," he explained with a wave, clearing plates from the table.

I nodded, wondering if this information would

34

prove useful later at some point during my investigation.

After thanking him for dinner, I volunteered to wash the dishes and do the cleanup. But once again, he refused. Finally, I retired to the camper. I fell asleep instantly, collapsing on my bed in the back. My sleep was dreamless for the first time in months. For that, I was grateful.

# CHAPTER FOUR

I woke up to a plate filled with farm fresh eggs and thick, crispy strips of bacon. "You're spoiling me, Bart," I said, accepting the plate gratefully. I stepped down from the camper. "I'm starting to think I'm at a bed and breakfast instead of doing real, actual work," I joked.

I took a seat on the second porch step and ate my meal as he watched me.

"I appreciate a good eater. My Mattie...she could put away some food. She was never a small woman, but I thought she was perfect," he said, a dreamy quality to his voice.

"She sounds like a wonderful woman."

"She was," he replied, mournfully.

Rays of sunlight spread across the farmland, creating an orange, pinkish glow over the dew-laden grass. It was a lovely place to wake up to, and since it was Wednesday, I knew that Mitch and Carmen would be working.

"May I speak to your staff?" I handed Bart my plate—it was wiped crystal clean after all that good food.

"Sure. Carmen is in the stables and Mitch is pulling up crops."

"Thank you for another delicious meal." I stood up, wiping my greasy fingers on the sides of my jeans.

The stable was massive, with eight box stalls on either side. I admired the horses, most of which were black and chestnut-colored. The white mare stood out like a sore thumb. Carmen was standing with her backside to me, bent over a large, green bale of hay. She placed a leaf of hay in a hay rack in one of the stalls. I didn't want to startle her, so I waited for her to turn around.

When she did, I was surprised by her beauty. A petite woman, not even five foot tall, her hair was the color of straw. She was dark-skinned with lovely facial features. Wrinkles around her eyes and mouth placed her age around forty.

"Hi. My name is Veronica von Derbach. I'm here to—"

"I know who you are and why you're here," Carmen said. The bitterness in her tone was undeniable.

'I hope you didn't come here solely to encourage these crazy notions of ghosts," she said, her Spanish accent more apparent as she spoke.

"That's not why I'm here at all, Carmen. I'm a psychologist who helps people who believe they are experiencing paranormal activity," I explained.

"So, then you *don't* believe him? Are you here to make him out to be a fool, then?" she demanded angrily. I could see that no matter how I answered, I couldn't win with this woman.

"No, not that either. I'm simply here to help Bart figure this out before he resorts to digging up his dead wife's body." I stared at her boldly.

She whipped back around, focusing on her hay.

"How would *you* explain his ghost sighting and the missing ring?" I asked gently.

"It's simple. He saw what he wanted to see. And he simply misplaced the ring." Carmen shrugged.

"But the ring is nowhere to be found and he doesn't strike me as a man with an overactive imagination," I said, trying to play devil's advocate. In truth, her theory was similar to my own.

"Maybe somebody took the ring. And maybe somebody really *was* out in the woods. The Tuttles live in a house out in those hills. Robert Tuttle has a young son and a teenage daughter. Maybe it was one of them out there," she said, chewing on her bottom lip as she mulled it over. Now this sounded like a bit of a lead.

"You said that maybe somebody stole the ring. Any idea who would do such a thing?"

"I don't steal," she declared, turning around to face me again and placing her hands on her hips. "I have three mouths to feed at home and bills out the wazoo. I would never risk losing my job with Mr. Eckleby over a stupid ring."

"I'm not inferring that you took the ring, Carmen. Bart said you're a reliable worker. I was hoping you'd also be a reliable source of information for me. That's why I chose to speak to you first."

At the mention of Bart's compliment—one he

didn't actually make—she dropped her arms to her sides, letting down her guard.

"Look, there are two teenagers that work here on my days off. They're punks, in my opinion. They always leave work behind for me and Mitch to finish. I wouldn't be totally shocked if it was one of them that took the ring."

I nodded, grateful for this bit of information. "I'll look into it. Thank you, Carmen," I said, making my way back out of the stable.

I had to walk a significant distance before I found my next suspect. Mitch was crouched down in a squatting position, yanking plump turnips out of sandy soil. "Hi, there. Veronica von Derbach," I said, offering my hand to him. I was determined not to rub him the wrong way like I did Carmen.

Mitch wiped the dirt from his hands onto his already dirt-encrusted shirt, and he gave my hand a firm shake. "Pleased to meet you, Miss von Derbach. I'm Mitch. I know you're here to help Bart, and I'll help anyway I can," he offered.

Mitch looked to be about sixty, with leathery skin and cornflower blue eyes. His hair was gray, but I could tell that he was quite a looker in his prime.

"Do you believe him?" I asked, getting straight to the point. Mitch winced.

"Of course I do. Bart and I...we've been friends our entire lives. I've helped him work these lands for nearly twenty years now. Like him, I'm getting up there in years. But I will work these lands until my back becomes crooked and my knees give out, because he's my friend and farming is all I've ever known." He looked off into the distance.

"Do you have your own farm?" I asked, not sure why I was being so nosy.

"Used to have a family farm about six miles from here but the bank took it," he replied, sadness in his tone.

"I'm sorry," I replied, regretting that I'd asked.

"The truth is, Miss von Derbach, Mitch has been misplacing things for months now. One day he can't find his plunger, and then the next he's lost his iron. I hate to say this, but I do often wonder if he's going a tad senile. I know he wouldn't make something like this up, so I do believe him. But I don't necessarily believe that what he believes to be true really is, if that makes sense."

It did make sense. "Have you seen anyone out in the woods behind the property?" I asked, tentatively.

"Never," he said.

# CHAPTER FIVE

This case wasn't moving in the direction I'd hoped, but lucky for Bart, I don't give up easily. After my conversation with the workers, I packed a small bag of stuff and headed off to explore the woods. If anything, I needed to go to the "scene of the crime," so to speak. I wanted to look for this supposed ghost on my own.

There was a heavily wooded area at the back of the property that extended into an upland plateau of hills. A narrow dirt pathway on the farthest east side of the tree line seemed like a pretty good place to start. The woods were filled with an ominous quiet, and the only sounds were the crunch of my sneakers on the twig-covered ground and birds chirping. The trees were so tall and their boughs so wide that they provided a type of canopy around me, blocking out the sunlight. The walking path was wide, but slightly overgrown, and I had to dodge limbs and thickets as I made my way through it.

I walked for nearly five hundred meters, scanning the landscape for some sign that someone

41

had recently occupied it. There were no fresh cigarette butts, candy wrappers, soda cans, or the like. If teenagers had been hanging out back here, they must have pretty neat and tidy ones.

I thought about Sully and the disturbing amount of clutter and garbage that always lay scattered around his bedroom. I used to hate cleaning his room. *What I wouldn't give to spend a day sifting through my son's trash again, if it meant having him back alive.*

A few more meters, and I stumbled upon a narrow creek bed. I squatted down to scrub the dirt from my fingers. The water felt strangely cool in this hot, muggy forest. I was nearing the end of Bart's property, and I scanned the hilly lands above me. I almost missed seeing the house on the hillside, as it was heavily camouflaged with its green and brown planking. If I hadn't been looking for it, the Tuttles' home that Carmen mentioned earlier would have just blended into the mossy vegetation.

The house was perched so high on the cliff that it appeared on the verge of toppling over at any minute. The view was frightening, and I simply could not comprehend why anyone would want to live so precariously. If I were a rock climber or even remotely physically fit, I would have tried to make the uphill climb. However, I'm neither of those things, so I had to come up with a safer route. *Surely, there must be a roadway that leads to it.*

I started the journey back to the farmhouse. Although I planned on conducting this investigation alone, I needed Bart's help with this.

# CHAPTER SIX

Despite the Tuttles' home's close proximity to the Eckleby farm, it took nearly thirty minutes to navigate the winding, hilly roads that led to its locale on the cliffside. Bart's directions had been clear and concise, and he'd even scribbled step by step instructions on a small piece of notebook paper.

I parked next to a hunter green BMW on the slanted driveway, and I remembered to use my emergency brake. I expected the house to look similar as it had from the woods, creepy and daunting, but it looked strangely serene from this viewpoint. There didn't seem to be any lights on in the house, but then again, it was early afternoon. I rarely turn on the lights when I'm at my apartment in the daytime.

As I stood on the flagstone walkway looking up at the house, I couldn't help but admire its enormous size. It had to be at least three stories high. I rang the doorbell and tapped my foot impatiently, trying to put together what I wanted to say. When a heavyset, burly man opened the door, I said, "My name is Veronica. I'm from Indiana. I'm traveling the globe, looking at some of the most splendid properties I can find in order to compile a list of my architectural favorites for *Better Homes and Gardens* magazine." I rushed getting the words out. *Sometimes I even surprise myself.*

He raised his eyebrows, but I kept rambling. "I was wondering if you might be interested in giving me a tour. I have a camera in my RV and I was hoping to snap a few photos." I added that part to make my story believable, but now I struggled to remember if my old camera really was in the RV…internally, I was kicking myself.

"Listen, I would really love to put your home in one of our magazines. I'm one of the top editors there," I pressed on. *I'm not an editor, and wouldn't it make more sense for me to say I was a photographer? Last time I checked, editors don't show up at people's houses to take pictures, nor do they turn up uninvited at someone's home.*

But it was too late to turn back now.

He squinted at the RV in the driveway. Like a psychic, I could read his thoughts. *What would a woman with a prestigious job working for* Better Homes and Gardens *be doing with a junky old camper?* he must be thinking. I was failing at this miserably.

"The camper has a lot of memories for me. My son and I bought it right before he died," I explained. It was the first truthful thing I'd said thus far, but I winced as I heard myself say it. *I can't believe I've resorted to playing the dead son card now*, I thought, disgusted with myself.

"I'm sorry," he said, his expression softening. "Lost my wife last year to cancer."

"Sorry for your loss," I said, suddenly feeling like a total scumbag. I wasn't even sure why I was here, or if this house on the hill had any connection to Bart's ghostly sighting in the woods.

"Come in," he said, pushing the door open behind him. I started to cross the threshold, but then he said, "Wait, what about the camera?"

I froze, remembering my lie from earlier. "Oh, y-yes," I stammered. I jogged back out to the camper, all the while praying that my old camera was still in the closet. It was seriously outdated and I'd been meaning to buy a new one since last year. "Please be in here. Please be in here. Please be in here," I chanted under my breath. I let out a sigh of relief as I uncovered the camera from under an old, musty set of sheets.

Mr. Tuttle was still waiting for me at the front door. "I'm Robert, by the way," he said, allowing me into his home. "It's not as tidy as usual. My maid comes on Thursdays, and since it's Wednesday…"

"Oh, that's okay, Robert. I'm looking at photos for architecture, not interior decorating," I assured him. I had to admit that every bit of this lie sounded ridiculous. Despite his warning, the handsome living room was immaculate. The inside decor seemed to match the woodsy design of the exterior. It had a rugged, log cabin feel to it, with a floor-to-ceiling fireplace and sturdy, wooden beams running across the entire length of the ceiling. There was even a deer head mounted to the wall. I remembered the camera around my neck, and I started snapping photos diligently.

Next, he led me into a kitchen and den, which were equally neat. I snapped even more photos. I felt slightly uncomfortable when he led me into the master bedroom, so I snapped the pictures quickly and backed out of there.

Finally, he led me up a winding staircase to the second floor bedrooms of his son and daughter. When I was outside, I'd been certain that it was a three-story home. But I hadn't realized how tall the ceilings were. His home truly did deserve its own spread in a top magazine.

"You know, you should invest in an updated camera," Robert said, pointing at my pitifully old-fashioned camera.

"I'm old fashioned, I guess." Changing the subject, I asked, "Are your kids home?"

He shook his head. "My son is with his grandma—my mom. She's got a big swimming pool, and I predict that my son will spend most of his summer there. My daughter is with her boyfriend," he explained, a look of disdain crossing his face.

The boy's room was decorated for a young child, with pictures of airplanes, baseballs, and monster trucks. "How sweet," I commented, snapping a couple of pictures. The girl's room definitely looked like it belonged to a teenager, with a collage of pictures on the wall and a makeup table covered in beauty enhancement items and jewelry. Even though it was a girl's room, it made me think of

Sully. *What would he be like if he was still alive? Five years can change everything...*

"Maddelyn will freak if a photo of her room is featured in a popular magazine. She'll be overjoyed when I tell her about you." He leaned against the doorframe with his arms crossed over his chest, a happy grin on his face.

Again, I was overwhelmed with feelings of guilt. I walked into her room and took nearly ten pictures. *Maybe I can send it in to a magazine for her anyway*, I considered.

"Do your children play out back much? I can see how you might be worried about them out there, since the drop off is so steep," I said.

"Never. I've always made them play in the front yard, even though it ain't much of a yard. My wife, she used to worry like crazy about them going out there, especially when they were little. When we bought this house we were childless. We didn't consider a family-oriented landscape. Perhaps we should have..." he said, rubbing his chin thoughtfully.

Coming here was starting to seem like a waste of time. Robert struck me as a good father, who didn't allow his children to venture down into the woods at night. It seemed unlikely that the so-called phantom was either of his children. And it couldn't have been the small boy; he would have fallen down the steep embankment running through the woods at night...

We headed out back and I now had the opportunity to enjoy the view from a different standpoint. I scanned the woods from above,

47

looking for anything suspicious, but saw nothing.

"Do you ever see any people or animals out here?" I snapped a few photos for myself. For the first time all day, I was actually taking photos of something that might be relevant to my investigation. I zoomed in the camera lenses, taking nearly a dozen close ups of the forest floor.

"Occasionally, I see deer and squirrels. But people? Never."

# CHAPTER SEVEN

I'd been hearing that word, *never*, a lot today. Although this case should seem cut and dried to me, I didn't have much to go on. Hopefully, tonight when I did my stake out, I would capture some sort of insight into this ghostly white figure in the woods. There had to be some sort of rational explanation for it all—there always was.

I dropped the photos I'd taken off at a local Smart Rite that offered one day photo developing. I'd been hoping for a time frame closer to one *hour*, but in a town this small, I'm not sure why I was surprised. While I was there, I picked up a bottle of red Bordeaux wine. It was the least I could bring, considering the fact that this was my third meal cooked by Bart in less than twenty-four hours.

When I returned, Bart was making a pot roast. Before I'd left for the Tuttle home, he'd reminded me that dinner was at four today. "Am I late?"

"Right on time," Bart replied, grinning at me cheerily from where he stood at the kitchen island, stirring something that smelled extraordinary in the crock pot. Mitch and Carmen were seated at the table, sipping glasses of iced tea. Mitch amicably gave me a little wave. Carmen, however, gave me a tight, slightly feigned smile. She was obviously not happy to see me.

I placed the bottle of red wine on the table, pretending not to see Carmen's scowl, and walked over to offer my help to Bart. As was becoming typical for him, he refused, encouraging me to sit down and relax with the others.

"How was your day?" I directed the question at both Mitch and Carmen.

"Fine," they answered simultaneously.

"How was yours? Find anything of interest?" Bart asked, raising his eyebrows in a hopeful expression.

"Not yet. I'm sorry," I said reluctantly.

Bart ignored my apology, placing juicy hunks of roast meat on clean white plates, and then surrounding the meat with round potatoes, buttered corn, green beans, carrots, and onions. It was your quintessential home cooked meal, and I couldn't wait to sink my teeth into it.

Dinner conversation was light as we all chowed down on the food.

"It's wonderful," I complimented Bart. He nodded a modest thank you.

He discussed aspects of the land and the status of the crops with Carmen and Mitch. They talked about farm work as though it were a science, and I enjoyed the way their conversation was both methodical and passionate at the same time. I suppose farming probably is a type of science, in its own way.

After dinner was dessert, a delicious blackberry and rhubarb pie. Bart even added a scoop of vanilla ice cream to top it off. His cooking was heavenly. My belly felt like it was on the verge of rupturing already, but I ate every single bite of the delectable dessert.

I knew it was probably a bad idea, but I let Bart talk me into refilling my glass of wine. We retired to a homey den that I'd never seen before. Carmen and Mitch thanked Bart for the meal, and told him that they would see him in two days.

I waved and flashed a big, bright smile at Carmen. She looked at me with disdain.

"Do you smoke?" Bart asked, catching me by surprise.

"It's been a long time, but I used to smoke occasionally in college," I admitted.

"Would you like a cigar?" He opened a small, wooden box filled with plump, sweet-smelling cigars.

*After so many indulgences tonight, why not?*

"Sure," I said, selecting one from the box. I let him light it for me, and I took a few tentative puffs. "I thought you only smoked outside." I raised my eyebrows at him as I puffed.

"Cigarettes, yes. But Mattie never minded the smell of cigars. She never smoked them herself, of course—that woman was a saint—but she would sit beside me, sucking in the fumes."

"It's good, right?" he asked, pointing at the cigar and smiling at me with another one of his self-satisfied expressions.

"Very," I admitted, taking a tentative puff.

There were several photographs on a nearby bookshelf of a lovely, silver-haired woman. "Is that Mattie?" I asked, standing up to take a closer look. He followed behind me.

"It is. She's a beautiful woman. *Was* beautiful," he corrected glumly.

There had to be at least twenty different framed photographs spread out haphazardly on the shelves. "Is this the ring?" I asked softly, noticing a picture of Mattie with her hands around her chin and a shiny ring displayed on her finger.

She had the most compelling hazel eyes. I almost got the sense that she was staring straight at me, into the heart of my soul. *Bring him some sort of closure*, I imagined her whispering. I tried to shake that thought away.

"Yes, that's the ring," Bart confirmed. The ring was silver with four tiny diamonds in its middle. I squinted at the photograph, taking in its details.

"I gave it to her on our twentieth wedding anniversary. I had it engraved with her name. It said, *I love you, Mattie*; simple as that. I couldn't think of anything grander to say, to tell you the truth. She was always the one who came up with brilliant things to say...not me..."

Bart cleared his throat, fighting off tears.

"I'm just so upset that it's gone because Mattie truly adored that ring. When I gave it to her, it had been nearly ten years since I'd bought her any jewelry pieces, and the excitement on her face when she opened that box, reminded me of when she was a young girl and we first fell in love. I'll never

52

forget the look on her face, like a kid on Christmas morning when she pulled off the paper and yanked the ribbon off. I don't know what she was expecting, but she didn't expect a ring. I fell in love with her all over again that day. And I think she did me too." His face puckered in pain and he stared at the threadbare rug at his feet.

"I will do everything I can to find it," I promised. My heart ached for this grief-stricken man. I understood his pain. I could only hope and pray that I could stay true to my promise, and solve this mystery for him.

# CHAPTER EIGHT

My camera may not be state-of-the-art, but my video equipment is nice. In the business that I'm in, I need an adequate video recorder to capture images of so-called ghosts. Perhaps I should get a better camera too, but I prefer to work with videos.

Still photographs of ghostly images leave behind too many unanswered questions. Such as, is that a ghostly orb or a particle of dust in the corner? To date, I haven't captured any ghostly images or video that were credible, or seen them with my naked eye, for that matter.

I assembled my tripod and placed the video camera carefully onto it. I opened up a lawn chair that I'd dug up from the RV, and plopped down into it lazily. It was going to be a long night.

The sun had edged its way down below the horizon, and nightfall was setting in.

I'd informed Bart of my plans to keep watch tonight. I'd almost expected him to insist on accompanying me, but thankfully, he just said "okay" and retired inside for the evening.

The wine and cigar smoke had made me a tad woozy, but I was determined to get some productive investigating done tonight.

Now that my video recorder was set into place, I settled into my steel-framed, semi-comfortable chair, and began the process of staring out into nothingness. My first case of the season seemed to be going nowhere, as much as I hated to admit it, even to myself. I'd done a few of these cases before, but now Dr. Paddison was sending me out with minimal supervision...I knew she was testing me, to see how I'd do in the field on my own.

The trees were shrouded in darkness, except for the natural light provided by a full moon. Its glow provided plenty of natural light to see a figure in the woods, even without porch lighting. Crickets were chirping and frogs were croaking, but besides that, the night was silent. It almost had an eerie quality to it.

In my line of work, I've heard a lot of complaints regarding eerie and uneasy feelings.

A "feeling," unfortunately, cannot be used as hard evidence when it comes to proving the existence of paranormal activity. However, I believe people wholeheartedly when they tell me this, and there actually is a grain of truth to these reported "feelings." The scientific explanation is that human beings can hear sounds up to twenty thousand hertz; anything below twenty thousand hertz creates "silent" noises that result in sound waves. How our body reacts to these sound waves, especially in the stomach area, can cause us to have positive or negative feelings for no discernible reason. Hence, some of these negative feelings can manifest themselves as feelings of unease.

A similar example of ghostly phenomena that can easily be explained is reports of so-called creepy drafts, particularly in old houses. Windows and chimneys, especially in historic houses, are usually the source of cold air. However, even in tightly sealed spaces, a process called convection can explain these drafts. When dry air sinks to the bottom of a room, the humid air rises, resulting in a small burst of cool air. And that's when you might feel one of these so-called "ghostly drafts." Mystery solved.

Hours passed, but nothing. No snapping twigs in the distance or suspicious shapes in the darkness.

The last time I checked my watch, it was three AM. I tried to stifle a yawn. I laid my head back against the now very uncomfortable chair, and closed my eyes for a few minutes. I needed a short break, that's all.

But the next thing I knew, I was drifting into another state of dreamless sleep...

# CHAPTER NINE

I woke with a start to the sun glaring in my eyes, burning the skin on my face. The grass was covered in dew, and based on the position of the sun, I knew it couldn't be much later than seven. *I can't believe I fell asleep*, I thought, cussing under my breath.

I folded up the chair, gathering my video equipment.

Bart was nowhere in sight, but I did spot two suntanned, shirtless boys baling hay in the distance. They paid me no mind.

I had a pounding headache, courtesy of last night's wine. Bart, with his wining and dining, was proving to be quite a distraction from my work…

I immediately felt guilty for blaming him. I simply needed to get to work. It was my responsibility to get this case resolved, no one else's.

I loaded the chair into a side compartment of the RV. Then I carried my video equipment inside. I needed to sit down and watch the footage. I didn't expect to see anything different than the nothingness I'd witnessed for the first half of the night, but I needed to be thorough.

Before I reviewed the video recorder's contents, I had to take some Advil for my hangover. If I let this headache go on much longer, I knew it would develop into a migraine, and a migraine could put me out of commission for the entire day.

Stupidly, I'd forgotten to pack any Advil in the small, compact medicine cabinet in the back. I momentarily considered knocking on Bart's door and asking for some, but then I would probably get stuck eating breakfast with him.

I could no longer afford distractions.

*I have other cases to get to, and I need to get this one figured out so I can move on.*

I jumped behind the wheel of the RV, and drove down the skinny, dirt road, which led me back into town.

I probably could have stopped at any convenience store or gas station along the way, but I opted to stick with the familiar, paying another visit to the Smart Rite. I grabbed a small basket, filling it with Tylenol, cold medicine, and antihistamines. I wanted to make sure this was my last stop for medications on my voyage across the country.

Even though it was early, and Pierce was a small town, I was surprised by the fact that there were no other shoppers in the store. The same girl who checked me out yesterday was standing at the register. The sight of her served as a reminder that I had pictures to pick up.

"I have a roll of film to pick up, also. Under the name von Derbach," I requested, loading up my items on the counter in front of me.

"Sure thing," she said sprightly. She sifted through a plastic bin of photo packets behind her, and considering the few that were in there, she found mine in no time. She sat it up on the counter, and rang up all of my items. I paid with a quick swipe of my debit card, and then thanked her politely.

It took a mere ten minutes to find my way back to the farm. I hoped and prayed for no interruptions this time. As soon as I was back in the back of the RV—with three Advil down the hatch—I hooked the video camera's USB cord into my USB port, and I waited for the video to load.

In the meantime, I ripped open the picture packet. I started sifting through the pictures nonchalantly as I waited for my expensive coffee-making contraption to finish its job.

The coffee came quick, thank goodness, and as I leaned at the counter taking small sips, I saw something that nearly made me drop the whole steaming cup on my feet.

"Oh my," I said, letting out a small gasp.

I finally had an answer for the mystery of Mattie's missing ring.

# CHAPTER TEN

I banged my palms on the Tuttles' front door, anger burning my face. I couldn't remember feeling this mad with any of my other cases. But Bart had left an impression on me, and I had a soft spot in my heart for him, perhaps because he had experienced a loss of his loved one recently, like me.

A girl around the age of fifteen swung open the door. She looked irritated by my presence on her front stoop, and her eyes were red with sleepiness.

"You're just who I wanted to see," I said, pushing the door open with my hand and stepping into the masculine living room that I'd just been in the day before.

"Hey! Who the hell are you, lady?" she shouted, swinging her long, blonde hair over her shoulder flippantly. "You can't just barge in here. My dad isn't even home. I'll call the cops on your ass!"

"Please *do* call the police. While you're on the phone with them, please let them know that they need to arrest you on theft charges."

"What are you talking about, lady? I've never stolen anything in my life! Is that why you're here? You think I stole something from you?" The girl was starting to look panicked, fearful.

Despite her worried expression, it was obvious she had no idea what I was talking about.

I let out a sigh.

When I was looking through the photos, I came across one I'd snapped of the young girl's dressing table. On it was one of those bizarre jewelry organizers shaped liked a dress. I didn't know what the ring looked like then and hadn't even considered it'd be on her dressing table, but the picture image didn't lie.

The same ring I'd seen last night in Bart's den had been hanging from one of the dress's small hooks.

I could remember focusing the camera on the jewelry organizer because I'd never seen one like it. Thank goodness I did, because I easily could have missed it.

Today the ring was not on the jewelry organizer because it was on her hand.

"That ring, there! It doesn't belong to you." I pointed at her left pointer finger.

She had a baffled expression…and I was starting to doubt myself…but then I remembered the engraving Bart had inscribed on it.

"Does it say *I love you, Mattie* on the inside of the ring?" Her already confused expression altered into utter wilderment.

"Of course it does. My name is Maddelyn. My boyfriend likes to call me Maddie, even though my dad hates it. He misspelled it, with two *t*'s instead of *d*'s, but I thought it was just a stupid mistake," she whined, sticking out her lower lip.

Suddenly, she looked less like a teenager, and more like a harmless little girl.

Now it was my turn to feel confused. "Your boyfriend gave you that ring?"

Her face suddenly paled. "Are you telling me that Sampson gave me a stolen ring?" she asked, on the verge of tears.

Sampson...I knew that name. Salazar and Sampson were the two teenage twins that worked on Carmen and Mitch's off days. *I guess Carmen was right about those boys, after all*, I thought wearily.

"Yes, sweetheart. I'm sorry to tell you this, but that ring belongs to Sampson's employer, Mr. Eckelby. That ring was an anniversary present for his late wife," I explained.

The tears were flowing now, and I suddenly felt awful for breaking this poor girl's heart.

"Honey, I'm sorry for coming in here and acting so harshly toward you. I thought you were the one who stole the ring, but now it all makes more sense," I apologized.

"How in the world did you know that I had this ring, anyway?" She was suddenly coming around and slowing her tears. Now she seemed a little suspicious.

I explained to her about my previous visit, and how I lied to her father. She looked at me like I was an alien. I can't say that I blamed her.

"Am I going to get arrested?" she asked dully,

finally bored with this drama.

"No, you're not in any trouble. But I would appreciate it if I could have the ring back." I boldly stuck out my palm.

"Gladly," she said, yanking it off her finger and holding it out to me, as though the mere sight of it made her physically ill. I plucked it from her fingers and shoved it into my jean shorts pocket.

# CHAPTER ELEVEN

Instead of confronting Sampson and ultimately, breaking the news to Bart, I wanted to finish watching the video and get my head on straight. Bart would not be pleased his employee was stealing from him, and I had to sort out how I was going to give him this news.

"Let's try this again," I mumbled, adjusting the coffee maker to fill a new, fresh cup. I selected an Irish Cream blend.

Perhaps this time, I would actually get to finish a cup.

With coffee in hand, I sat back down at the wobbly RV table and pressed play on the video. I let it play for nearly twenty minutes, sipping my coffee, before I started to scan though it slowly. I looked for any changes in the landscape.

About an hour in, I hit pay dirt.

There was a flash of white skin and long hair darting from left to right. I stopped fast forwarding, and I watched it at normal speed.

Then I watched it again in slow motion.

It was official: I could finally identify the white-colored ghost.

# CHAPTER TWELVE

I needed to talk to Bart, but instead I began browning ground beef and a roll of sausage in separate skillets on the stove. I softened lasagna noodles and mixed a pre-made, Italian sauce on the stove.

Lasagna has always been my comfort food, and it's one of the few things I can cook well.

My mother died in a car accident when I was seventeen. Her death was not instant. My father and I spent nearly six days waiting by her hospital bed, watching her fade away. It was painful. And it was slow.

The hardest part was there was nothing we could do to help her. I felt powerless.

My father and I were so accustomed to my mother taking care of our food needs that we barely ate all week. On our first night home after her death, my father sifted through cabinets in search of something good for me and him to eat. Finally, he settled on making lasagna.

After losing my mother, the last thing I wanted

to do was eat. But when I took a bite of that delicious pasta, a warm sensation rolled through my body, and I ate until my belly ached and I felt the urge to lie down and take a nap. I knew my mother was with me and my father would take care of me. I say "I knew she was with me," but that's when I was young and idealistic, and I believed in silly things like that...

But ever since that day, I'd always prepared lasagna in times of stress. It had been Sully's favorite too. Today, I was making it for Bart, because I knew he would take the news I was about to give him hard. Like me, he wanted desperately to believe his late wife was still with him...

After covering the layers of noodles with my spicy mixture of cheeses and meats, I wrapped the top with foil and slid it inside the tiny camper oven.

It only took thirty minutes to bake, so while it was cooking, I took a few final notes and sent Dr. Paddison an email.

*I'm leaving for Nebraska tonight*, I wrote.

# CHAPTER THIRTEEN

Bart was pleasantly surprised by my conciliatory lasagna. I had my laptop in one arm, and the heavy glass pan in the other. "Let me help you with that," he offered, relieving me of the pan. When I set the computer down on the dining table he said, "I guess we're talking business." He scratched his chin nervously. Deep in his heart, maybe he already knew how this was going to go...

"Let's eat first," I suggested.

Bart oohed and aahed over the lasagna, making a big show of his appreciation. I was grateful for his kindness. I'd never been so fond of one of my clients before. It was an unfamiliar, yet pleasant, feeling—to care so much for the people I served. I'd shut myself off from the world after Sully...and letting myself care for someone felt strangely good, and normal.

Once our bellies were full, I opened up the computer and pulled up the video clip.

"There's no easy way to say this, Mr. Eckleby..." He raised his eyebrows.

"I mean, Bart," I said apologetically. When it came to delivering my final results, I couldn't help but maintain an air of professionalism.

"Please, just watch the clip," I said finally, turning the screen toward him.

He watched it, his expression changing from hopeful to confused, and then to solemn. He let out a long whistle.

"I can't believe Brownie got out," he said softly.

"Brownie? You call your *white* mare Brownie?" I asked, unable to contain my amusement.

He shrugged, grinning sheepishly, his shoulders relaxing. "I have a sense of humor. At least I used to…"

He stared down at his worn out fingers, shaking his head.

He looked up—there was that hope again. "But wait. What about the ring? A damn horse can't stroll into my home and take my dead wife's ring!"

I slid the small, brown envelope across the table. The expression on his face when he saw the ring inside was a mixture of relief and sadness. He wasn't ready to give up on the hope that his wife was visiting him from the dead.

"But…how?" he asked, twirling the tiny ring on his pinky finger. I told him everything. About the lie I created to get into the Tuttle house and his employee's thievery.

"I can see why Sampson thought the ring would be perfect for her since her name was Maddelyn. But you know what's sad? If he just would have told me the truth, I would have advanced him the money from his paycheck to go buy one for her.

Hell, I might have even just given this one to him!" His eyes were watery, full of disappointment.

"Will you fire him?" I asked, pretty sure I already knew the answer.

"Maybe…maybe not." He rubbed his face in his hands. "I'll definitely give him a stern talking to." He stared out the window at the two boys hard at work. "I'm so sorry, Veronica. I wasted your time. I can't believe I was actually going to exhume my wife's body. Truth is, I just wanted a chance to see her again. I hate the fact that she's lying there in a bed filled with filth and worms. She would hate it down there," he croaked. The dam broke, tears spilling over.

"With all due respect, Bart, be glad that you have a grave to visit for your wife. My son's body has never been found, and his grave remains empty. I would give anything to have a proper resting place, a place where I could mourn him."

I don't know why I mentioned Sully. It was inappropriate and out of the blue, but it felt good to share it with someone who could relate to my pain and anguish. And I wanted him to find a way to see a brighter light in all of this…

Bart looked at me in surprise. "What happened? To your son, I mean?" he asked, reaching out for my hand.

I didn't want this to turn into a sorrow fest for me, not when he was the one that was supposed to be the client. But I told him everything anyway. It seemed therapeutic for both of us.

"Thank you for sharing your story," he said when I was done, standing up to give me a hug. I nodded, accepting his embrace awkwardly.

"I left you a list of referrals for therapists who specialize in grief counseling. There are also several groups within fifty miles of here that meet weekly to discuss loss." I pointed to the paper on the table.

"Also, the neighbor behind you—Mr. Tuttle—he recently lost his wife to cancer. It wouldn't be a bad idea for the two of you to talk."

"Thank you," he said, reaching out to shake my hand. I turned to leave, but then I had another thought.

"Bart? You really should consider opening a bed and breakfast. You are a splendid host and cooking seems to be your number one form of therapy."

"I'll consider that," he replied, grinning from ear to ear. I turned to leave, pressing my hand on the doorknob.

"What is your form of therapy, Veronica?" he asked from behind me.

"To search for things unseen. To prove to myself he's gone, I guess..." I admitted, surprising myself with the words.

As I pulled away from the Eckleby farm, I watched Bart's figure grow smaller and smaller in my rearview mirror.

Case one was officially solved.

# CHAPTER FOURTEEN

If you follow the gnarly, twisted branches of my family tree, you will discover that the von Derbach family has a history of knighthood that traces back to the 13th century. My family name is associated with the craft of witch hunting, and my distant ancestor, Balthasar von Derbach, was a Benedictine monk who was recognized as a witch hunter in the 1500's.

Balthasar played a significant role in the deaths of 250 people accused of being witches—my bet is that all 250 were innocent.

Although this part of my family history is filled with the type of violence I'd never condone and am not particularly proud of, I do often wonder if my destiny has always been to hunt paranormal creatures.

*Veronica von Derbach, the modern day witch hunter!*

All jokes aside, I take my job seriously and I'd like to think I'm reversing the family's bad name by hunting down *actual* paranormal creatures—and ultimately, proving they don't exist at all. Because let's be real—they don't. If someone who investigates this type of thing on a regular basis can't find *anything* to prove ghosts exist...well...

The country landscapes blurred through my periphery as I made my way to my next destination of Cheyenne, Wyoming. It was time to meet the Rockford family.

Jodie and George Rockford were tax preparers who shared two children, ages fourteen and six. Within the past year, their youngest child, a daughter named Suzie, had begun having bizarre night terrors. According to her family, Suzie often had inexplicable bruises and scratches afterwards. And according to Suzie, a demonic creature was coming into her room, causing the marks on her body.

I drove to the rhythm of the Heartbreakers, letting Bart's question roll around, permeating my thoughts. *What is your form of therapy, Veronica?*

I didn't know the answer, honestly. Sometimes the so-called "experts" in the fields of social work and psychology are the worst at dealing with their own issues. We use others to heal ourselves, which is a big "no-no" called transference.

I'm just as guilty as everyone else in the field, I suppose...

\*\*\*

After eight hours of driving, I was welcomed by the beautiful Black Hills, and ultimately, the city lights of Cheyenne. Compared to the sparsely populated town of Pierce, it was swarming with people and traffic, even though it was already ten PM.

I'd called ahead and spoken to Mrs. Rockford, so she was aware of my late arrival. I'd offered to park the RV overnight, and wait to conduct our initial meeting in the morning, but she'd insisted that I come on in, since nighttime is when most of Suzie's reported demon sightings occurred anyway.

The Rockfords lived on the second floor of a modern looking brownstone building. It was at least ten stories tall. *Not your typical haunted house.*

There was a parking garage attached to the building, equipped with its very own guard shack. The stocky young guy who manned it had been told to expect my arrival, and he let me in without any questions.

I found an empty spot large enough for my RV on the ground level, nervous I'd scrape the roof against the low ceilinged parking garage. Satisfied with my parking, I made my way back out in the dark, eager to speak to the Rockfords.

I let myself inside the brownstone, then checked in with the attendant at the front desk. He ushered me into an elevator, and I rode up to the second floor, wringing my hands impatiently.

The hallway was silent, and I stood outside the door of the Rockfords' apartment. I felt awkward. I didn't want to wake up the kids.

But simply just standing here wasn't much of an option either...

I looked up and down the hallway, feeling nervous. Although apartment buildings and condominiums don't normally give me the creeps, deserted hallways do. I blame that on Stephen King's *The Shining*. My mom let me watch it when I was eight and I was permanently scarred because of it.

I bit the bullet and rapped on the door lightly. A few short moments later, a tall, elegant woman who looked like a runway model opened the door with flair. A short, chubby, balding gentleman peeked out from behind her.

They both looked stressed beyond belief. "Please come in and take a seat, Mrs. von Derbach," the woman—who I assumed was Jodie Rockford—said, leading me to a stiff, fancy loveseat that sat in the center of an odd-shaped, contemporary living room.

A kitchen and dining area flowed straight through it. Besides the closed bedroom doors lined up down a short hallway, the entire space was wide open.

I took a seat. Jodie and George took a seat in the two armchairs across from me. They worriedly looked at each other, then looked back at me.

"Please bring me up-to-date on what has been happening to your family," I said, pulling out my pad of paper and pen. My scribbling from my visit with Mr. Eckleby covered the first several pages in the notebook. I felt a pang of guilt for leaving so quickly—I really liked Bart.

I flipped to a fresh page.

"Suzie has always been a normal child. *Better* than normal, actually. She excelled in kindergarten and was always ahead of other kids her age when it came to developmental milestones. She's never had

75

any physical, mental, or emotional issues up until this point. That's what you want to know, right?"

Not waiting for me to answer, she said, "I've been trying to pinpoint a trigger for when all this started, but honestly, there isn't one. Six months ago, she woke up, screaming and shaking uncontrollably. It took hours to calm her down. She claimed that a demon with sharp teeth and hands came into her room and held her down on the bed. She said that she couldn't breathe and she thought the monster was going to kill her. Of course, we tried to tell her that there's no such thing as monsters, and that it was only a dream. But one week later, it happened again. And then again and again. It's the same story every time. The demon. She thinks there's a demon in our house." Jodie let out a loud whooshing breath, her face taut with worry.

I nodded, encouraging her to go on.

"After a while, it started happening every night. Only recently, one of her teachers from school contacted us to tell us that Suzie had strange bruises and abrasions on her. The private school we send her to is very prestigious, and they didn't want to call Child Protective Services. However, they were concerned and wanted to discuss it with us. When we asked her about the marks and examined them ourselves, she claimed the monster did it. She denies doing it to herself and we would never harm our child."

"Has she been to see a therapist?" I asked, setting my pen down.

"Yeah. She has a psychiatrist. He diagnosed her

with early onset schizophrenia and prescribed her a cabinet full of antipsychotics. We've been giving her the medicine as prescribed, but it hasn't been helping. She still has the dreams every night and sometimes she still has strange marks. She was once a happy girl and she has become depressed, agitated. Reclusive. She doesn't act like our little girl anymore...and then the other day, her psychiatrist recommended inpatient hospitalization. I don't want my daughter on a psych ward, Mrs. von Derbach."

It was the second time she had used the 'Mrs.' suffix, but correcting her now just seemed plain rude. I asked for the name and contact information for Suzie's psychiatrist, and I jotted it down hastily. I also made a list of all of her medications and dosage levels.

"Any recent issues in the family? Have you guys had any marital problems or have there been any recent deaths in the family?"

They were routine questions for a case like this. "You sound just like *her*," George muttered, and I knew he meant the psychiatrist.

"I'm just asking some standard questions before I begin my investigation. I am in no way trying to blame you guys or belittle the problems that Suzie is having," I assured him.

"*She* said that too," George said. His chin drooped down, resting on his chest. This man clearly felt defeated.

His wife shushed him and answered 'no' to all of my questions. "Any problems at school before this?" She shook her head. "What is your son's name and age?" I pressed on.

"Timmy. He's fourteen. He's a great kid, and despite their age difference, they have always gotten along beautifully. He was excited about having a sibling and he cares about his little sister's well-being very much," Jodie answered.

"Has *he* had any mental or behavioral problems?"

Once again, the answer was no.

"They are both well-adjusted children. Well, until this happened with Suzie."

"I've seen her drawing of the monster. Do you know where she says the monster is coming from?" I asked seriously.

"She doesn't say," Jodie answered, shaking her head back and forth.

"Do her night terrors occur at the same time every night?" I asked.

"It's at least a few hours after she's gone to bed, but sometimes it's in the middle of the night or mid-morning," she explained, wiping at the corners of her eyes with a soft tissue.

"May I sleep on the couch this evening? I'd like to stay close so I can be of assistance and talk to her directly after the nightmares occur." I set my notebook aside.

For the first time all night, both parents said, "Yes," in unison.

# CHAPTER FIFTEEN

I glanced at the clock on the Rockfords' living room wall. It was a bizarre-shaped clock that created the illusion that it was melting. It reminded me of that painting by Salvador Dali, *The Persistence of Memory,* and I wondered if that's what its maker was going for.

*Time, how it doth persist indeed*, I thought, settling down on the loveseat with the pillow and quilted blanket that the Rockfords had given me.

Despite the loveseat's sleek design, it was an uncomfortable old thing.

It was only eleven. I was usually more of a night owl, but tonight I truly was exhausted. I pulled the covers up to my chin and flipped out the small desk lamp beside me. Within minutes, I was sawing logs.

Like most nights, I dreamed of Sully and that dreadful day at the lake. Even in my dreams, the tragedy felt like it happened just yesterday. I stared at the empty seat on the boat. *Come back. Oh, please come back.* And then time moved backward—I saw his smiling face and rosy cheeks, riding along on the tube.

If only I'd known that a short while later, he would plunge into the stormy waters and suffer an untimely death...

Some nights, I dream that I'm swimming underwater, searching for him wildly like I was that day. But other times, I dream that I find him down there, and I see his bloated cheeks and bulging eyes...

*Why did you leave me down here, all alone in this dark place?* his corpse often asks me.

I awoke for a second, but then I settled back into a sleep filled with roaring waves and sharp boat edges.

Finally, I jerked awake—to the sound of a little girl's piercing scream.

I noted the time for future reference. It was 2:15 AM. Since I had yet to meet Suzie, I didn't want to panic her more by walking into her room. My initial plan was to simply observe how the Rockfords handled the situation.

The two parents darted out of their rooms, one after the other, and raced into their daughter's bedroom. A lanky, spiky-haired teenager opened the door of his bedroom and padded across the hallway to join them. I stood toward the edge of the doorframe, observing the family in action.

Suzie continued to scream while her brother stood back observing and the parents comforted her on the bed.

Jodie clasped the tiny, petite girl in her arms, stroking her hair and humming. George offered words of comfort. "It's okay, honey. You're safe here. It was just another dream," he whispered from the bed.

"I couldn't breathe again. It was squishing me!" Suzie proclaimed. When her mother tried to remind her that it was just a dream, the little girl became defensive.

"He was in here! It wasn't a dream! I was awake. If you all don't do something soon, he's going to kill me!" she warned them.

Jodie looked up at me, her eyes pleading.

When Suzie became sufficiently calm, I stepped into the room and approached the bed, moving slowly.

"Suzie, my name is Veronica. I help people who think they can see ghosts and monsters. May I sit down and talk with you?"

The darling child was clutching a dingy, old stuffed rabbit to her chest. She looked nervous but nodded, her chin still trembling as though she might begin crying again.

"May I have some time alone with her?" I looked back and forth from Jodie to George. They looked hesitant to leave their young child with a stranger, and I can't say that I blamed them.

"Sure," George finally replied, kissing his daughter on the top of her soft auburn hair. Her brother, Timmy, hung back as though he hated to leave his sister's side.

Jodie gently nudged him away from the bed.

Jodie, George, and Timmy stepped out of the room, and Jodie pulled the door shut behind them. "You must be so scared," I said to Suzie, looking at her sympathetically. She nodded, clutching the rabbit tighter. There was a plastic Barbie chair fit for a young girl, and I pulled it up beside the bed, squeezing my bottom into it awkwardly.

"When the monster was lying on top of you, were your eyes closed?" I asked, my question quiet and slow. She hesitated, clutching the rabbit tighter. But then she nodded, a nervous smile on her lips.

"Will you tell me what happened *before* he got on top of you?" I asked. Again she hesitated.

"I know it's scary to talk about, honey. But I promise I will keep you safe while I'm here. I come from a family of monster hunters. I know how to deal with these types of things." I sat up straighter in my chair, trying to look tough for once.

It was a half-truth. My long distant relative, Balthasar, was probably no more than a murderer of innocent people. But I needed some leverage here. "Really?" she asked, incredulously.

"Really," I said.

She nibbled on the rabbit's ear for a moment before she said, "I was asleep. I was dreaming that I went to a cool cottage in the middle of a flower garden. The cottage had cookies and candy in it," she said, as she slowly began to recall the dream.

"But then I sat up in bed because I heard someone at my door. I saw the knob turning, but before I could scream, the monster swung open the door and flew over to my bed. That's when I couldn't breathe," she said, a tremble in her voice again.

I could tell that her heart rate and breathing were picking up again, and I had her do a few simple breathing exercises. "Remember that you're safe because I'm a monster hunter," I reminded her, teaching her to breathe with only her nose and release the air through her mouth.

"Now, I want you to think about the monster on top of you, when you couldn't breathe. I know your eyes were closed, but what could you feel him doing?"

"He was breathing on my neck. And his face was covering my mouth," she squeaked.

"What part of his face was covering your mouth?"

"*His* mouth," she responded finally.

"And tell me—what were his hands doing?" I asked next.

"Touching my body," she admitted.

I could tell her anxiety was increasing again, but I wanted to keep her talking while I had the momentum going. "What part of your body was he touching?"

"Everywhere!" she shouted unexpectedly. I put a finger to my lips. I wasn't ready for Jodie and George to coming charging in here yet.

I reached out, petting the toy rabbit in her hand. "What is your rabbit's name?" I asked, trying to help her relax.

"I call him Tender Bear," she said sweetly, a smile forming at the corners of her mouth.

"Do you and Tender Bear do a lot together?" She nodded excitedly.

"We like to pretend to eat sandwiches together. Sometimes we even make up entire worlds together! And we like to play on the merry-go-round at the park. Tender Bear always falls off and gets hurt. But I know how to be a doctor, so he's in good hands with me…"

"Poor Tender Bear! Does he get boo-boos often?" I was happy to see this conversation leading back in the right direction. Again, she nodded.

"What about you? Do you ever get boo-boos, Suzie?"

She immediately stiffened. *She's a smart girl*, I realized. *She knows when I'm asking relevant questions…*

"Suzie, this next question is very important. It's like playing pretend, just like you and Tender Bear do…I want you to pretend that the monster turned into a human. Who would he turn into, do you think?"

She looked at me, her eyes wide with fear. "Can monsters turn into people?" she asked, and her voice was trembling with fear.

"No, Suzie. But sometimes people can act like monsters. Who do you think the monster would turn into if it could? If we were playing pretend?" I asked, unsure if I was handling this properly. "My brother," she whispered, glancing at the bedroom door fearfully.

# CHAPTER SIXTEEN

It took less than thirty minutes to extract a confession from the boy. Apparently, there was a forty-five minute window on weekdays, where Timmy was watching little Suzie until his mother arrived home from work. It was during these short gaps of time that he was molesting his little sister.

Poor Suzie was suffering from post-traumatic stress, and during her night terrors and flashbacks, her attacker was manifesting himself as a monster with a disgusting mouth and hands. My heart ached for the girl, and what would happen next to her family.

I contacted the proper authorities, which were the police and social services. I waited for an officer to arrive, and I broke the news to Jodie and George Rockford while their children sat separately in their own respective bedrooms.

They were horrified, angry, and disbelieving. But most of all, they were pissed at me.

I wasn't offended. I know what it's like to not want to accept the horrible truth, especially when it comes to your own children.

The police arrived quickly, and without any warning, which I was grateful for. They spoke to me first.

The parents were in no mood to take my advice, but I did tell the officer that the number one priority was getting the entire family into counseling, and treating Suzie for PTSD immediately. I wasn't sure what would happen to the boy exactly, but I had a pretty good idea.

I left for my RV before I had to witness a young boy placed in handcuffs.

I knew the Rockfords would be traumatized by their son's arrest, but he was still alive—unlike Sully—and that meant there was still time to save him and their daughter too.

# CHAPTER SEVENTEEN

I tossed and turned all night, drifting in and out of sleep. I dreamt of Sully, as usual, but I also dreamt of the girl. I dreamt of faceless demons with sharp claws and teeth like she described, chasing me down the highway relentlessly. I woke up with a start, sitting up in the bed, confused about where I was at first. I glanced over at the bedside clock. It read 4:46 AM. I groaned.

I like to get up early, but not this early. I considered lying back down, but I felt too wired and anxious from the dreams to do so.

I got up, stretched, and gathered up clothes and a towel. *Nothing like a five AM shower*, I thought, grouchily. I stripped out of my pajamas, and stood under the showerhead, trying to enjoy its lukewarm temperature and pitifully low water pressure.

I thought about my dreams. Running down a deserted highway, demons chasing me ceaselessly...it didn't take a psychology degree to figure that one out.

*No matter how far I go or where I run off to, I*

*always feel like I'm alone and the demons of my past still follow. I've never gotten over my son's death, and perhaps, I never will.*

I stepped out of the shower, shivering, and I dried off as quickly as possible. I tugged clothes on over my still-damp skin, and ran a comb through my hair. My hair was such a dark shade of brown that it could almost be considered black. It's not straight, but it's not curly either. It's that sort of hair that lies there limply, in oddly angled waves of fury.

I consider drying my hair, but it would take forever with my travel-sized blow dryer. I used a towel to soak up some of the water, and then twisted it up into a loose, wet bun on my head. *Since I'm up this early, I should hit the road. There's no use in making the mayor wait.*

But I was hesitant to skip town just yet. I needed to check in with the local Cheyenne police department. It's possible they'd need me to stick around to answer more questions regarding the Rockford case. *It's a bit too early to call the station*, I decided, slipping on my oxford flats.

The parking garage was fairly well-lit, but it was still pitch dark as I stepped out onto the city street. The same young man from earlier was posted up at the guard shack, but instead of guarding, he snored softly with his head tilted against the glass window at an odd angle.

It was summertime in Laramie County, but it felt more like fall, with a cool, morning breeze blowing across my still-damp hair and clothes.

Strolling down the main street of Cheyenne, I kept an eye out for oddballs. The street mostly deserted, I spotted a few grungy stragglers and a pair of drunken school boys. No one seemed to pay me any mind.

I passed by nearly a dozen closed businesses, not looking for anything in particular...just walking, blowing off steam.

Restless, I stopped in front of a peculiar-looking store, adorned with green bottles of "magic herbs" in the window.

"A cure for anything!" boasted a weather-faded sign hanging from the shop window.

*I wish*, I thought, grumpily.

I'd walked so far and now the main street was reaching its end. The streets up ahead weren't as well-lit.

*What am I even doing out here, walking alone in the dark?* But then I saw it, the park Suzie mentioned earlier.

It seemed so out of place near the city street, but it looked like any other normal park. It was a nice, roomy patch of grass situated between two buildings. I strolled over to it, walking through grass so high that it brushed across my calves, wetting them with dew.

I reached down with the tips of my fingers, enjoying the cleansing feel of the wet blades.

There were two swing sets, a rickety old slide, and a merry-go-round, just as Suzie described. It looked ancient, like it'd been painted over ten times.

I took a seat on the rotating platform, soaking the butt of my pants in the process. I didn't care at this point; every other part of me was wet.

I spun around slowly, using my feet to power the

old creaky thing, thinking about Sully when he was little. He loved the park, and he especially loved merry-go-rounds.

I wish I could say that I have all these memories of taking him to play on one and doing so many fun things, but I was always so busy with my work.

We didn't do enough of the simple things, like visiting parks, for instance.

*I regret that. I regret so many things...*

I wasn't ready for the tears to come, but they came anyway. They spilled over, drenching my already wet face and shirt, and I finally gave up fighting. I sat there for nearly an hour, sobbing into my hands, whispering apologies to my long lost son.

It wasn't the first time I'd cried since his death, but it was the first time I'd cried those sort of tears, the kind that take your breath away and are impossible to stop—a good, ugly sort of cry.

By the time I finished, my face was puffy but dry, and the sun was peeking out over the horizon. The streets were slowly coming alive, and a few passersby were staring at me strangely.

I started the long walk back to the RV.

I had a job to do. Maybe I couldn't save my son, but I could still help others in their time of need. It felt good knowing someone needed me; it filled a tiny space in the huge gaping hole in my chest— that was saying something. I suppose that that's my answer—*helping others instead of focusing on myself is my own twisted version of therapy.*

# CHAPTER EIGHTEEN

It was a lengthy drive from Cheyenne to Lansing, Michigan, which is where Mayor Ron Fish resided. The last thing I did before I left Wyoming was check in with the local police department. They assured me that I was good to go, and they would contact me if necessary.

I felt like something was missing, like I should be doing more for the Rockfords...but my job was to figure out who or what the demon was that was terrorizing little Suzie, and I'd done that.

I drove for nearly fifteen hours, stopping once only to pee and grab a small bite to eat. Even after all that driving, I was still a few hours away from my destination.

Finally giving in to the exhaustion and hunger pangs, I parked for the night at a rest stop in Ohio.

The rest stop was mostly filled with truckers, but I saw a few hookers too.

Grabbing a stale pack of jelly donuts from the vending machine, I opted to get back in the camper, locking my doors up tight.

It was nearly midnight, and I had a long day ahead of me in the morning, but I sat at the table wide awake, scarfing down the donuts, swigging from a hot two-liter bottle of Pepsi. The drive had left me feeling famished. A rush of sugar usually did the trick for me...

In between bites and sips, I took out my paperwork on the Mayor Fish case, and scanned through the information. The mayor had a lovely, supportive wife of twenty years and two teenage boys, ages fourteen and seventeen. Up until six months ago, life in the Fish family household had been not only normal, but great, according to Mayor Fish and his wife, Aimee.

The problems started when they purchased a new home in the Greenbriar Golf Community. The house they purchased wasn't old, not by any means. There was only one previous owner, which was a family that lived there for two years and went bankrupt. No one died in it, or in the houses surrounding it, according to the Fish couple.

Despite all of that, they were reporting objects flying around the room—plates, knick knacks, chairs—all by themselves.

This falls into a category of ghost behavior known as a "poltergeist."

The word 'poltergeist' is actually a German word, meaning "noisy ghost." So, any ghost who is responsible for causing physical disturbances, like moving furniture or objects, would be classified as such.

Not only were the Fish family reporting the movement of small objects, but they were also reporting levitated chairs, shaking of light fixtures, and strange, ghoulish sounds at night. On all accounts, it sounded legit.

I sat at the table chewing on my pencil eraser, considering possible causes of poltergeist activity. The idea of invisible hands moving stationary objects was difficult for anyone to explain.

Last year, I'd had a case that involved shifting furniture and dishes, but it all turned out to be a direct result of seismic activity in the area. With that in mind, I pulled out my outdated laptop and I searched for any news articles or other recent reports of earthquakes in Michigan.

None could be found.

My next concern was that the paranormal events were being created by someone in the house, or someone who seriously disliked the mayor. Considering the fact that he was approaching his next election and there were thousands of local residents with the potential for disliking him, there was no easy way to narrow down a suspect. Not yet, anyway.

Finally coming down from my sugar high, I stretched out on my bed, propping up the pillows beneath me.

I considered other possible explanations for the Fish haunting, but kept arriving at a dead end.

*There is the one explanation…that there really is a poltergeist haunting the Fish family. But…I don't believe in ghosts.*

# CHAPTER NINETEEN

The Greenbriar Golf neighborhood is a gated community. I felt like I was visiting a prison as I waited for approval to come inside.

Finally, the beady-eyed, lip pursing lady who guarded the entrance pressed a button, lifting the guardrail to let me pass. I rolled my eyes in the rearview mirror.

I'd never been a fan of cookie cutter McMansions, but I had to admit that Greenbriar was lovely. It was a beautiful spread of well-conditioned grass, with breathtaking, massive homes dotting its lawn, and a million dollar view of the Great Lakes on its outskirts.

I saw the unmistakable flagsticks pointing up from the ground. Greenbriar's resident golfers were out in full swing, either carrying golf bags, swinging clubs, or gliding across the course in their golf carts.

With few trees around for shade, the course was so white bright that it nearly blinded me. The rundown RV looked ridiculous in this environment, but I parked it next to the curb in front of the Fish family home.

Standing in front of the three story home, I admired its Goliath-like size and immaculate front lawn. The grass was an unbelievable shade of green.

I pressed the doorbell, waiting patiently. In a house this grand, I half expected a maid or butler to greet me. But it was the lady of the house, Aimee Fish, who answered, dressed in her finest aerobics gear.

"Hi, there!" she greeted me amicably. She let me in, all the while using the towel around her neck to wipe away the sweat from her face.

"Hello. I'm Dr. Veronica von Derbach," I said, nodding pleasantly. I figured if I started with the doctor part, maybe it would stick for once. Everywhere I went, everyone called me "Mrs.," even those who knew I was a doctor. My male counterparts in grad school never seemed to have this problem...

I followed Mrs. Fish through the foyer and past several fancily decorated living room spaces. A living room, another living room, and what appeared to be a decent-sized library. "This is it. The room where the stuff was being tossed around," she said matter-of-factly, leading me into a twelve by eight dining space.

The area was filled with an antique dining table that held enough placements on it for twenty people. The only other piece of furniture in the room was another antique: a hutch made of timber, designed with ornate scrollwork and an assortment of fancy drawers, shelves, and cabinets. It was filled with china, pictures, and old fashioned figurines of little girls and teddy bears. My mind drifted back to little Suzie…

"This belonged to Ron's mother," she said, pointing at the hutch. "She passed away last year, which is when we inherited it. Honestly, I hate the old thing, but Ron just can't seem to part with it. I've begged him to give it to charity." She sniffed, looking at the hutch with disdain.

I narrowed my eyes at this woman. She was staring at the family heirloom like a piece of worthless trash that belonged in a homeless shelter.

I ran my hands along the hutch's sleek veneer, remembering one I'd seen once at my paternal grandmother's house. It was a beautiful piece, but nowhere near as fancy or valuable as this one. "I love it," I admitted, smiling at her apologetically.

"Thank you, dear!" boomed a loud man's voice. I nearly jumped right out of my skin. I turned around to see Mayor Ron Fish in the flesh, staring at me appreciatively. "At least someone around here has a little taste," he said, winking at his wife.

"I'm Ron Fish," he said, gripping my hand so tight that it hurt. I introduced myself, and asked if we could sit and talk.

Ron motioned for us to sit at the dining table. I pulled out one of its high-backed, heavy chairs and sat down. I pulled out my notebook and pen.

Before I even had to ask, Ron launched into his story of the Fish family poltergeist. Boisterous and red-faced, he waved his hands around as he talked.

"Not only has someone been throwing items off of this shelf, but we've seen it with our own eyes.

Miss, we have a serious ghost problem here. I hope you're equipped for the job! I pray you brought your holy water, and all that."

He looked from me to the notebook, waiting for me to write something down. I started scribbling down a few notes to appease him.

"Explain the occurrence in detail," I urged.

"The first time it happened, we were right here, eating dinner at the table. We were midway through our meal when a candle holder in the shape of a cherub came flying straight at my head. A cherub. Now don't you think that's significant?"

I stopped writing, my pen poised mid-air.

"You actually *saw* the candle holder fly off of its space on the hutch and hurtle toward your seat?" I asked incredulously. I hated to sound like a cynic, but that's exactly what I was, and this story sounded like a lame version of The Amityville Horror.

"Well, I didn't *see* the entire occurrence the first time," Ron admitted. "I was eating chicken Florentine when I saw a strange, white blur fly past my vision field. It was an inch away from my face, and it crashed into the wall over there, breaking into pieces. It was my mother's favorite candle holder," he said ruefully.

"I'm sorry, Mayor Fish. I know that must have been frightening. Did anyone else see it?" I asked, trying to stay patient.

"I did," Aimee said, finally joining the conversation. "And my oldest son, Adam, was sitting at the table too."

"The very next night, it happened again, only this time, the spirit broke four of my mother's favorite teacups. One of the cups struck Aimee in the back. She wasn't harmed, but after that, I knew who the spirit had to be," Ron said matter-of-factly.

Again, I stopped writing, unable to hide my expression of surprise. "You think the spirit is someone in particular? I thought you said nobody died here?"

"Oh, no one died here, Miss. But the owner of that hutch is deceased," he said, pointing his chin in its direction.

"You think the poltergeist is your *mother*? But why would she torment her son and grandsons?" I asked incredulously.

"Not *us*. *Her*," he said, pointing a finger at his wife.

"Oh, I see," I said, holding back a smile. "Your mother-in-law and wife didn't get along while she was living?" I asked, catching a glimpse of Mrs. Fish's eye rolling routine in my periphery.

I couldn't blame her for being irritated with her husband. The idea sounded ludicrous, if I did say so myself.

"No, they never got along. In fact, they hated each other. My mother could never come between us in life, and I think that's why she's wreaking havoc now. Plus, she knows that Aimee hates her precious hutch and its valuables," Ron said, maintaining a serious demeanor.

"Do you or Aimee have any other enemies you can think of? Someone who might have a motive for disrupting your lives?"

"Oh, yes!" Ron declared, chuckling. "My arch-nemesis, Tom Seagull, is running against me for office. He definitely has a reason to try and destroy me. But that's not what's going on here."

"Anyone else?" I pushed, making sure to note Mr. Seagull in my notebook.

That definitely seemed like an avenue worth exploring.

"Well, there are plenty of people, ma'am. People who don't agree with my policies, especially those who are rooting for Tom to replace me."

I didn't tell him this, but I completely agreed. Politicians always have enemies; it comes with the territory of the job, I guess.

"Any names, besides Mr. Seagull?" I asked. I stared at the name, *Seagull*, on the notepad in front of me. I stifled a laugh. I imagined a loud, gray bird swooping down to eat its meal: a juicy, plump fish. Seagull and Fish running for office. I wondered how long it would take for the papers to make that analogy.

"Veronica? Are you listening?" Ron asked, raising his eyebrows peevishly.

"I'm sorry. I'm just reviewing the details," I lied.

"This poltergeist is my mother. And we need to put her to rest, somehow or some way…"

"Now, Mrs. Fish, do you have any enemies that come to mind?" I turned to look at Aimee.

"None that I know of. I'm home most days. The only time I go out is to shop or do my aerobics," she admitted.

"And the boys? Any conflicts at school? Or friends they've had a falling out with?"

She thought about it for a minute, but then shook her head firmly.

"Besides the items flying off the hutch, what other strange things have happened?" I asked, flipping to a fresh sheet in my notepad.

"Chairs lifting by themselves and strange moaning sounds at nighttime," Ron replied, popping the knuckles on his hands nervously.

"Which chair was it?" I asked, glancing at the chairs around the table.

"Not in here. Upstairs in my son's room."

"Your oldest son, Adam?" I asked curiously, setting down my pen and stretching my own fingers.

"Nope. It was my youngest son, Flynn. He's fourteen. He was upstairs in his room, typing up a paper for school. He got up to turn on his printer, and that's when the chair lifted up from the ground, and fell back down on its side," Ron explained.

"Did it only happen that one time?" I asked.

Aimee chimed in: "No. It happened a handful of times, all while he was doing his studies in his room."

"If the entity is your mother, how do you explain her terrorizing your son? That doesn't sound like something a grandmother would do."

Ron chuckled, leaning back in his chair. "With all due respect, you don't know my mother. She was a spiteful woman, and when someone wronged her...well, let's just say, she never forgot about it. My oldest son, Adam, was a dutiful grandson. He visited her on the weekends, and entertained her jokes and eccentricities. But my youngest was never too close with Mom. He only went around her when we forced him to, and he avoided her like the plague. I think that he thought she was weird. My guess is that she resented him for this, and now she's toying with him, getting a little payback," he explained.

*Wow, what a nice grandma!* I thought sarcastically. If the Fish family really was experiencing acts of a poltergeist, I prayed it wasn't Grandma Fish. She sounded scarier and more spiteful than any other "normal" ghost.

"You said you have proof?" I asked, trying to hide my skepticism.

"Oh, yes!" Ron announced proudly. He stuck his hand in his pocket, coming up with a sleek, black iPhone.

"We got the ghost on video!" he revealed. I couldn't believe it. I'd never seen an actual video of a ghost. *Was it possible that they'd really caught one on film?*

# CHAPTER TWENTY

Considering that the video had been recorded with a mobile device, I was shocked by the quality. I reminded myself to get an iPhone the next time I went in to Verizon for a phone upgrade...

The video itself was approximately three minutes long. At first, when it started, I couldn't see much of anything. But then the dining room came into focus, crystal clear, in fact. I could see Ron and Aimee, sitting calmly in their chairs, eating their evening meal. They obviously were not the ones who were filming.

"Keep your eyes focused, peeps! You are about to witness something amazing: the wrath of the Fish Family Ghost!" a young boy's voice declared. I looked up at the couple quizzically.

"That's our Flynn. He's a little dramatic," Aimee whispered.

The boy went on talking for several more seconds, telling the audience about their recent paranormal experiences. Suddenly, he focused the camera on the hutch.

Moments later, I was shocked to see a tiny dog figurine pop up from where it sat on the shelf and drift closer to the videographer. It seemed slow and ghostlike, floating in midair held by a set of unseen hands.

I'd never seen anything like it. I edged my face closer to the screen, trying to understand how it worked. This couldn't be real, could it?

I jumped back, startled as the object in the video flew right at the videographer's screen, marking the end of the video.

I let out a deep whoosh of breath. "Wow. That was pretty disturbing," I admitted. Ron and Aimee were smiling, with looks of self-satisfaction. They thought I believed them. Hell, maybe I even did.

"I'd like to speak with the boys, if that's okay with you."

"Sure, but right now they're out skateboarding with a few kids from the neighborhood. They should be home in a couple hours. In the meantime, may we show you around and take you to your room?"

Out of habit, I started to turn down her offer of giving me a room for the night. The RV was sounding pretty good right now. But considering these reports and the ghoulish nighttime sounds, I figured it was probably a pretty smart idea to stay inside the residence.

Ron and Aimee led me around the house and property, giving me a tour that I thought would never end. Their house was massive, with eight bedrooms and six bathrooms, as well as an assortment of bonus rooms. It was a gorgeous home, but I couldn't imagine having to clean and maintain such a large space.

"Do you have a housekeeper?" I asked, looking at Aimee. Surprisingly, she shook her head. "Sometimes I hire cleaners to help with my big jobs, but I do most of it myself. Like I said, I don't work, so I have the time to do it."

"What she really means," Ron chimed in, "is that she likes to do things her way. She doesn't want any housekeepers around, or they might mess with her pretty things."

Aimee nudged him, trying not to smile at his joke. I could see that despite their bickering, this couple truly had a lot of affection for each other.

Finally, they showed me to my room, a lovely space nearly triple the size of my bedroom at home. There was a soft-looking, queen-sized bed in the middle, and an assortment of shelves, dressers, and bookshelves.

I stood at the shelf, appreciatively scanning the book titles. They certainly had great taste in literature, which made me like them more.

The shelves contained some of my favorites: *Jane Eyre, To Kill a Mockingbird,* and *Frankenstein,* to name a few. *Well, at least I have something have to keep me entertained tonight if I get bored,* I thought happily.

# CHAPTER TWENTY-ONE

The boys returned a few hours later, toting skateboards under their arms. I introduced myself to them, then asked similar questions to the ones I'd asked Ron and Aimee. They were quiet, but pleasant. They answered my questions, but offered nothing new to the investigation.

I told Aimee and Ron that I had to run into town, and I loaded into the RV, pulling away from the Greenbriar community—which was starting to feel more like a resort.

I couldn't imagine living somewhere like that. With the outrageous mortgage payments and property taxes, I probably didn't want to.

I drove only a few miles to reach my destination. Tom Seagull's headquarters were located in the center of town, and they were smack dab in the middle of a cluster of other businesses and small specialty shops. Parking the RV was going to be a total pain, I realized. I finally found a parking lot

105

two blocks away, and I sauntered back in the direction of Seagull's office.

By the time I arrived, I was out of breath, red-faced, and sweaty. *Maybe I need to take some aerobics classes myself*, I thought, opening the front door.

There was a pretty young girl at the front counter. She didn't look a day over eighteen. "Hi, there! I'm here to see Tom Seagull!" I announced cheerfully.

The girl didn't buy my cheerleader routine one bit. She narrowed her eyes and asked, "Who are you, and what do you want to talk to him about?" I'd been expecting this, and I had a story planned out.

"Okay, the truth is, I'm a reporter. But I'm a huge fan of Mr. Seagull's, and I'd really like to do a piece on him for the paper," I lied.

"And what paper is that again?" the girl asked, picking at her perfectly manicured nails as though I was too boring to be bothered with.

*"The Number One Scoop*," I told her proudly. She stopped rapping and looked up at me.

I'd done my homework. After the *Better Homes and Gardens* incident, I came better prepared this time.

*The Scoop* was Lansing's number one ranked magazine for young adults in the area. I flashed her a wooden smile.

The girl stood up, smoothing her wrinkle-free skirt. "Okay, so here's the thing. Mr. Seagull has left for the day. But he'll be back in the morning. Would you like to see him first thing?"

"That would be wonderful," I replied, that awful smile still plastered on my face.

"How about seven?" she asked eagerly. Now that she thought I was from a prestigious paper, she was treating me with respect, which really got under my skin.

"See you then," I said, winking at her conspiratorially.

\*\*\*

I made it back to the Fish residence just in time for dinner. I wouldn't normally dine with my clients—Bart Eckleby was an exception—but dinner was part of the job in this particular case. Considering the fact that most of the poltergeist phenomena was happening in the dining room, sticking around seemed like a smart idea.

Aimee had prepared a health-conscious meal of beets, carrots, and a small piece of baked salmon. I tried not to show my disappointment as I took tiny bites of the bland food.

On my way back from Mr. Seagull's office, I'd spotted a pizza place. *I wonder if they deliver*, I thought, chewing the tough carrots and counting how many chews it took to get it down.

The entire family was at the table: Mom, Dad, and both boys. I sat in silence, letting them carry on as usual.

They discussed sports, recent events, and celebrity gossip. I watched the boys, trying to imagine Sully at their age. *I wonder if he would have liked skateboarding,* I considered thoughtfully.

107

Dinner lasted for nearly an hour, but there were no signs of a ghost. Ron and Aimee seemed disappointed.

"Mom is being shy tonight," Ron said, laughing to himself. Aimee and the boys rolled their eyes at each other, obviously not believing Ron's theory that the ghost was their dead grandmother.

"Does the ghost normally act out every night, or does it just occur randomly?" I asked, looking back and forth between the family members.

"It's a spotty ghost, that's for sure," said the youngest boy, taking a sip of his water. "Sometimes things happen several days in row, but then other times, a week passes by in between occurrences."

For my sake, I hoped that I didn't have to stick around for a week to find out. I had other cases to get to.

I was still tired from my travelling, and I decided to head to bed early. I read a few pages of *Mansfield Park* by Jane Austen, which I'd never read before. The book was interesting, but my eyes were heavy, and I drifted to sleep.

I woke up a few hours later, unsure what it was that stirred me from sleep. I sat up in the dark room, listening breathlessly. I'd expected to hear strange, ghost-like moaning as they'd reported. However, what I heard instead were sounds of movement above my head. The guest bedroom I was using was on the second floor, so it had to be someone, or something, in the attic. I imagined fat rats or possums.

I strained my ears, trying to hear it again but was met with complete silence. I slipped out of bed, creeping toward the doorway to the room on my tip-toes. Suddenly, I heard a creepy, inhuman scream, "Get out of this house!"

I jumped out of sheer terror, running for the door this time. I threw it open, racing down the stairs crazily, slipping on a few steps at the bottom.

"Are you okay?!" Ron shouted, arriving to the hallway with a shotgun by his side. Aimee was right behind him. It took me a moment to catch my breath, but when I finally did, I told them about the terrifying voice in my room. "You all didn't hear it?" I asked, shocked.

"It didn't sound male or female, just creepy. Almost demonic. If I had to pinpoint the sound, I would say it came from above," I said, more to myself than them.

The three of us flipped on lights, and cleared each room—one at a time. The boys had joined us now, and they also helped search the rooms.

It took nearly an hour to go over the huge space with all of its rooms, and when it was over, we'd found nothing on the first two floors. The house seemed to be free of any human predators, which meant the voice came from the Fish family ghost.

I still wasn't sure I believed it, but I tried to be as open as possible. I felt certain that there was still a reasonable explanation for all this. I just needed to figure out what it was.

# CHAPTER TWENTY-TWO

I barely slept a wink all night, lying on top of the covers in the guest room with the lights in the room shining bright. I was grateful when morning arrived.

In the camper, I dressed quickly, eager to meet Mr. Tom Seagull this morning.

I arrived at 6:55 AM, waiting patiently in his lobby. He was nearly thirty minutes late, much to his secretary's dismay.

When he got there, she looked embarrassed but he made no apologies. He ushered me to the back, a cramped office space. His desk was covered from one end to the other with law books and folders filled to capacity.

"Are you a lawyer?" I asked, glancing at the mountain-sized books on his desk.

"Is this the interview?" he asked gruffly, taking a seat behind his desk.

I took a seat on the other side, leaning forward so that I could peer over the tall stack of books to see his face. He frowned.

"Yes, I have a law degree. But I'm making a run for mayor. This town needs a new leader who will fight for better paying jobs and clean up these disgusting streets."

I took out a small handheld notebook and a stubby pencil—I had to at least pretend to be a reporter.

"Mr. Seagull, I must admit that I'm not a huge fan of our current mayor, Ron Fish. That's why I'm here—I'm excited about having a new candidate to consider, especially one with an impressive educational background such as yours." Batting my lashes, I prayed he would fall for my act.

His frown faded and he smiled, showing me two perfect rows of pearly whites. He wasn't a bad looking man, but he had this air of aristocracy about him that seriously turned me off.

"I would love to hear about your background and qualifications for the position of mayor," I said sweetly. That was the last question I had to ask because he started blabbing—for what seemed like hours.

He talked about his early "good ol' boy" days in college and his endless lists of organizations and honors. I tried not to let my eyes glaze over, but after a while, I started to tune him out. I wrote furiously, feigning interest.

By the time he was done, I had pages filled with nonsense, illegible scribbles, and bird drawings.

If truth be told, after hearing all of Tom Seagull's qualifications, it was hard to argue that he wasn't fit for the job. I suspected that Mayor Fish was going to get a run for his money come election time.

"Is that enough information for you?" Mr. Seagull asked, his voice bursting through my scattered thoughts. "I have an appointment at 8:30." He glanced at his watched, suddenly bored with talking about himself.

I'd gain no information about his relationship to the current mayor, which was my entire premise for requesting the interview.

"May I ask one more question?" I asked sweetly.

"Sure, make it quick," he said, standing.

"For all of the voters out there who think Mayor Fish should stay in office: why do you think he should be replaced?"

He smirked. "That's the easiest question of all. Because I'm better!" he boomed, then started laughing, his thick, bulky shoulders shaking with his chuckles. "I went to school with ol' Fish Face, and we lived only a few blocks apart. Even from an early age, we were always at each other's throats, a good old fashioned rivalry. We competed at sports and with our grades. We even fought over the same girl."

Mr. Seagull must have sensed my curiosity, because then he said, "In case you were wondering, I got the girl." He tapped at the wedding band on his left hand.

"It sounds like you guys hate each other," I said, prompting him for more. He smiled sadly. "Nah. There's just something about the relationship between a man and his arch enemy. They are always connected in a strange sort of way, and after a while, they start to respect each other..." I could sense that he was talking about himself and Mayor Fish. This guy was definitely not our poltergeist. *What a waste of time*, I thought, pushing my notebook into my messenger bag.

"But those boys of his," Mr. Seagull continued, "they are simpletons."

That statement struck me as odd. "Why do you say that?" I asked, puzzled by his point of his view.

"Well, my son goes to school with Ronnie's boys, and he's always coming home, talking about this or that, one stupid thing they've done after another. Like, for instance, the Fish family supposedly has a ghost problem."

Of all the statements I'd expected him to make, bringing up the ghost wasn't one of them. According to Aimee and Ron, the whole thing was supposed to be hush-hush. In fact, Mayor Fish has specifically requested that I avoid talking to reporters, or telling anyone about the unusual ghost activity.

*How did his running mate know about the poltergeist?*

"Why do they think it's a ghost?" I asked, pretending to be ignorant about the situation.

"Well, the boys captured an invisible phantom throwing around stuff in their house. They posted the video on YouTube, and it's gone viral. Nearly six hundred thousand views, according to my son. You see, those boys are strange. While ol' Fish Face and I were challenging each other on the ball court, those boys are stuck behind their computer screens, making up stupid stories about goblins and

113

ghouls. I'm sorry, but I'm late for my appointment now."

I thanked him for the interview, and darted out of there, eager to check out this video on YouTube. I was certain it was the same one they'd shown me the other night, but regardless, Mayor Fish was going to be livid when he found out.

# CHAPTER TWENTY-THREE

I stood in the lobby of Peggy's Pizza Parlor, waiting for my extra-large pizza to arrive. The smells of the restaurant invaded my senses, making my belly rumble. By the time it was done, I was half-tempted to throw open the box and eat some right there in the waiting area, but I forced myself to wait, carrying it out to the RV. I loaded up my laptop and got my pizza ready before settling down at the table.

I nibbled at the delicious, gooey pie as I did a Google search for YouTube videos involving ghosts. I found it within seconds.

*A Real-Life Poltergeist in Lansing, Michigan*, the title read. I watched the short clip a few times—it was the exact same one I'd seen on the mayor's iPhone.

It wasn't hard to figure out why the boys put it online. They were getting a lot of positive attention because of it, as evidenced by the hundreds of comments written below it. They were essentially online superstars, approaching a million hits on their video.

I groaned. Did I really have to be the one to tell Ron and Aimee about their sons' wrongdoing? *No*, I decided. *I'm here to find ghosts, not get teenage boys in trouble with their parents.*

I stared at the video, noticing the username written below. It read: *Posted by The Abra Cadabra Brothers.*

It seemed like a strange username for the boys.

*Abra Cadabra, a magician's term.*

I had a fleeting memory of myself as a child, doing god awful magic tricks in front of an audience made up of bored family members. My Aunt Irene bought me a book and a box set of "tools for conducting magic"—as the print on the front proclaimed. I never could master the tricks; either my hands weren't fast enough, or I'd forget a step or two mid-trick.

It is a magician's job to create illusions, using deceptive devices or sleights of hands. The posters of this video obviously considered themselves magicians.

I was flipping through The Abra Cadabra Brothers' YouTube channel when I discovered a case-breaking clue.

# CHAPTER TWENTY-FOUR

Here's the thing about YouTube: When you have your own channel, subscribers can see all of your videos. Let's just say that looking at videos titled, *How to Create the Illusion of Objects Levitating*, seemed more than a little suspicious. These videos were far less popular and older, but they were there nevertheless...

There were also nearly a dozen Halloween videos, compilations of "haunted sounds" for people who wanted to design their own haunted houses. I played the Halloween clips and heard the typical sounds one would expect from a ghost: moans, groans, and grunts.

Apparently, a single person could use cheap, invisible wire you can buy on the internet to create the illusion of objects moving on their own. My guess was that the boys were slipping the wire through the vents in the dining room ceiling and connecting them to their grandmother's knick

117

knacks and dishware when their parents weren't around.

I sighed. I finished my pizza, but I was barely tasting it now. I cleaned up afterwards, and then drove to the Fish family home.

It was late afternoon, the house completely deserted.

I saw it as an opportune time to explore the vents in the dining area, and the contents of the hutch more closely.

Scooting one of the heavy dining room chairs over, I used it to get closer to the vent. Sure enough, there were tiny, little remnants of barely visible wire looped through its slats.

The boys had recently used scissors, or a knife, to cut away the access string, but they hadn't been thorough. There were still tiny traces of the string on the vents and around the heads of a few small figurines. I snapped a photo of the wire around the vents, and I slipped the figurines into a Ziploc bag for evidence.

I headed back out to the camper, feeling satisfied that the case was solved. The floating objects could be explained, as well as the ghostly sounds. *They even tried to scare me away with that creepy voice*, I thought, shaking my head as I remembered the cruel words. Those knuckleheads were in so much trouble!

I couldn't help wondering about the floating chair though…I thought back to what Aimee and Ron had told me, I remembered one very important fact about their story. Flynn had been alone when this phantom chair rose from the floor and fell in his room. Considering everything else, I knew it was most likely a lie.

Perhaps he and his brother were hoping to pull off a chair levitation, but weren't quite skilled enough yet. My guess was that, like most boys their age, the boys just wanted attention. *Maybe someone should have bought them a magic kit when they were little*, I thought, fighting back laughter.

They'd accomplished notoriety on their YouTube channel and they'd grabbed their parents' attention. After all, their father was a politician, and most likely wasn't around as much as the boys would have liked. I felt sorry for them—I honestly did. But their actions were still pretty boneheaded.

At least in *this* case, the ending wasn't tragic.

I was eager for the Fish family to get home so I could report my findings to them, and then to Dr. Paddison.

It was time to get debriefed on my next set of cases and I wondered what would come next. *Maybe this next one will be near the beach*, I thought hopefully.

*A headless phantom wanders the shore, requiring me to hang out on the beach all day. Now, wouldn't that be perfect?*

I didn't expect the Fish family to come back for hours, so I decided to take a nap until they did. After so many restless nights and a full drive ahead of me, I needed the rest desperately.

# CHAPTER TWENTY-FIVE

I'd planned on contacting Dr. Paddison when I'd finished up with Mayor Fish, but she surprised me by calling me first. My eyes were still squinted with sleep as I stumbled around the cramped camper space, trying to find my cell phone. I finally spotted it next to the coffee pot, and I grabbed it before it could stop ringing.

"Hey, Dr. Paddison!" I exclaimed, putting on my most cheery voice. I wasn't looking forward to breaking the news of how the police had to get involved in the Rockford case. At least the mayor's case was going to be resolved pretty painlessly. The boys might be grounded for a while, but that seemed pretty minimal compared to the alternative: a real-life, scary ghost or someone suffering abuse like poor little Suzie...

I answered the phone, eager to fill Dr. Paddison in on my recent cases. But before I could even begin, she said, "We need to talk, Veronica."

Conversations that begin this way are usually serious, and most unpleasant. I braced myself.

"Okay," I said, taking a seat at the table because there was nowhere else to sit but the bed.

Dr. Paddison said, "I had a case come in this morning. I thought you might want to take a look at it."

"Okay," I said, opening up my notebook, prepared to take notes. Dr. Paddison released a heavy breath.

"A woman faxed me a picture of a ghostly image. All I have is her address and name. The image is of a young boy standing in a heavily wooded area. The picture is very faded but it does look rather odd. The woman swears that she snapped the photo right before the ghostly apparition disappeared."

"Is that it? I will be more than happy to look into this, but shouldn't the cases you already have lined up take precedence?" I was confused—why was this new case important? I didn't play favorites with Mayor Fish; and I wouldn't be starting now.

But I could see why this was interesting...a ghostly image caught on camera was unusual...but more than likely, this one would turn out to be the result of a hoax, glare, or camera malfunction. Or a simple childish trick, like with the Fish boys.

"Well, there's something about this case that I want you to know. It comes from Lake Merlott." Her voice was barely above a whisper now.

For a moment, there was nothing but silence in the air between us. I realized I was holding my breath.

"Let me hook up my fax machine. Fax the image over to me in five minutes," I instructed, already unloading the heavy machine from a cabinet above my head. "Make it three minutes," I said, then I hung up.

I plugged in the fax machine, loaded it with paper, and turned it on. My brain was on auto pilot.

I made sure my settings were adjusted correctly, and then I tapped my fingers on the table, waiting impatiently for the image to come through.

After what felt like hours, the machine came to life and an image began to transmit through, albeit at the pace of a snail.

"Come on!" I screamed at the machine. Finally, the image was almost complete…

I yanked the sheet from the tray, immediately lifting it up to the light.

I gasped and placed a hand on the table to steady myself.

There was no doubt—the boy in the picture was Sully.

# CHAPTER TWENTY-SIX

Lake Merlott is in the state of Kentucky. In order to get there, I had less than a half day's drive back in the direction I'd come from originally. Neither distance nor time mattered to me; I just had to get there.

I'd left the evidence of the invisible wire, as well as screen shots of the YouTube videos and links for Mayor Fish. I called him and told him that I had an emergency, but that his case was resolved, and I'd locked the materials for him in his office. He seemed satisfied with that. I told him to call me if he had more questions. I didn't expect I'd be hearing from him any time soon.

I filled up my tank at a hectic gas station right outside of the city. Before leaving town, I contacted Detective Lackey again at the Laramie County Police Department to make sure they didn't require anymore statements regarding Timmy Rockford.

Thankfully, Timmy had also confessed to

Detective Lackey and his deputy.

"What will happen to the boy?" I dared to ask.

"He'll be tried as a juvenile. With cases like this, the defendant usually takes a plea deal. He might do some time in a juvenile detention center, and he will certainly be placed on probation. He will also become a registered sex offender." I cringed.

"And Suzie?" I asked.

"She's been admitted for psychiatric treatment at Lily Andre's Treatment Center for Children. They are one of the most prestigious centers in the nation, and they will help treat her symptoms before sending her home," he answered.

I thanked him for his time and assistance with the case, and I hung up the phone. I dialed information and tracked down a florist, so I could send flowers to Suzie's room. Once that was done, it was finally time to drive to Lake Merlott.

My mind was still spinning from the photo I'd seen. *Maybe I'm wrong*, I thought, but then I looked over at the picture sitting on the passenger seat, and then to the one on the dash. There was no doubt about it. It was Sully.

I tried to examine it objectively, as though it were not my son. "What do you see, Veronica?" I asked myself out loud. *Be the doctor, not the mother of a lost son...keep your cool.*

The picture was a black and white shot of a boy standing in the middle of a forest. The expression on his face was blank and mildly frightening. He was wearing jeans and a dirty t-shirt, with his hands held straight down at his sides. I didn't recognize the clothes, but since the photo wasn't in color, I couldn't really identify them anyhow.

It looked like my son. It looked like Sully.

In the picture, he looked to be the same age that he was when he died. *My number one theory is that this is a hoax of some kind. But why? And who would do such a thing to me? I don't have any enemies. Is it possible that one of my past clients is pissed at me and playing a trick, some photoshopped image...?* But I'd never told any of my clients about my son. Except Bart Eckleby. *But why would he send this?* And it was a *woman* on the phone, according to Dr. Paddison.

I'd called Dr. Paddison back and demanded she give me every detail of the situation, but she had few to provide. A woman who identified herself only as Aubrey said that she took the picture at Lake Merlott. The address provided was unfamiliar to me, but I knew it had to be close to the lake and campground.

I hadn't returned there since the last search team scoured the water and surrounding woods for Sully's body. That was nearly five years ago.

I never planned to return there. But that was all about to change.

# CHAPTER TWENTY-SEVEN

Besides one pit stop for gas and soda, I drove straight through to Lake Merlott. It was nearly two in the morning when I approached the old, familiar guard shack that I'd seen countless times as a child, and with Sully that last summer.

I was surprised to see a gray-bearded man manning the shack. I wouldn't swear to it, but I almost thought he might be the same gentleman that sat in the booth five years ago when Sully and I checked in. I don't know why, but that thought alone gave me the creeps.

"How do ya do, ma'am?" he asked sleepily, tipping his hat. I surprised myself by saying, "I would like to reserve lot sixty for the next three days."

He fiddled around on the computer for several seconds, before giving me a price. I paid the seventy-two dollars. He handed me a reservation pass to hang on my mirror, and I thanked him before pulling away.

Although it was officially summer, there were only six other campers taking up spots. No idea why I chose to stay in this spot again. It was my father and Judy's old lot they reserved, and it was where I spent my last night with Sully.

*I guess if I'm hunting for Sully's ghost, I might as well go to where he might be. I can't run away anymore...*

I pulled into the camping space and parked in the same location that I did five years ago. The only thing different was that I was alone this time. No Dad. No Judy. No sisters or bubbly, bouncing babies. *No Sully.*

After that summer, my father and his wife, who used to love camping, never went again, at least not that I know of. Dad also sold the boat. He never went out on the water again...

After nearly fourteen hours of driving, I was absolutely famished. I didn't have any wood yet to build a fire, so I dug a pack of bologna and cheese out of the refrigerator. I put together three sandwiches, and then I carried them outside. I plopped down on the one metal step that extended from the door of the camper. I had a lantern somewhere, but I was too hungry and tired to go digging for it. I sat in the darkness, waiting.

I was waiting for my dead son.

# CHAPTER TWENTY-EIGHT

Aubrey Chetfield lived in a miniature mansion that overlooked Lake Merlott. Its size made Robert Tuttle's home resemble a small trailer. The house was surrounded by a heavily wooded area that led to a dock on the water.

It wasn't far from where we parked the boat that dreadful day when Sully wanted to fish.

*Was it truly possible that my son's ghost was haunting Lake Merlott? But I don't believe in ghosts—do I? Is it possible that I've been wrong all along?* I chewed on my lip anxiously.

Ms. Chetfield was expecting me, but I don't think she was expecting to come face to face with the supposed ghost's mother...

The house was glamorous but the woman who answered its door was anything but. Aubrey Chetfield had dull, colorless hair and eyes, and she wore a perpetual frown. She looked like a homely woman who'd had her fair share of bouts with depression.

"I'm Veronica von Derbach. Pleased to meet you," I said, shaking her hand cordially. She opened the door and I followed her back outside onto a luxurious balcony attached to the back. From here, I had an amazing view of the sparkly, still waters of Lake Merlott.

*It's hard to imagine that these same calm waters devoured my son and ruined both of our lives in an instant.*

I took a seat in a stiff plastic chair, and she did the same. "So, you're basically a ghost hunter?" she asked, staring down into the thick trees and brush that led to that horrific water.

"I guess you could say that. I have my doctorate in parapsychology. I investigate paranormal phenomena," I explained blankly.

"But?" she asked, as though she were reading my mind.

"But…" I said, "this case is different. Because the boy in the picture you sent is my son." I expected her to look surprised, but her face didn't change and her eyes didn't move from the tree-lined water.

"I know who you are, Veronica. I saw you on the news. *All* of us around here followed the coverage. I prayed every night—I prayed they would find your boy. But I knew they'd never find him."

"Why?" I asked, suddenly confused by this meeting and by her odd behavior.

"Because none of the other children that disappeared from here have ever been found," she said, glaring at me with an ominous expression.

# CHAPTER TWENTY-NINE

"What on earth are you talking about? No one ever mentioned other missing children," I said, my voice shaking. There was a cramp in my stomach and I felt as though an enormous boulder had been placed on my chest. I tried to draw in deep breaths but couldn't.

"That's because they didn't go missing all at once. I've lived in this lake town my whole life, and over the past fifteen years, a handful of children have gone missing. Boys and girls, all of them between the ages of twelve and seventeen. Every couple years, it happens again," she said, finally turning to look at me.

"Kids drown. It happens all the time. It happened to my son," I declared, sticking out my chin defiantly.

"Perhaps you're right. Or perhaps the lake is claiming victims. Maybe it's a curse. Or maybe there is something more sinister going on. All I know is that your son is dead or I wouldn't have seen his ghost."

Her words were cold and cruel. They felt like sharp daggers jabbing into my heart. I already knew my son was dead. I didn't need to be reminded. I had the urge to jump out of that chair and smack her across the face. Better yet, I'd like to throw her off the balcony. *How about that for a curse?* I thought angrily.

I stood up to leave.

"I'm sorry if what I'm saying hurts you. I sent the picture because I thought you deserved to see it. Nothing more, nothing less," she called out hoarsely from behind me.

I slammed the door on my way out.

# CHAPTER THIRTY

Sheriff Billy Joe Baggins hadn't changed a bit. He was still pushing three hundred pounds, and he still had a mushed in face that resembled an ugly pet shih-tzu.

When I stormed into his office, he was eating a double with cheese and drinking a Big Gulp soda. His expression went from startled to confused to agitated, and then finally softened as recognition kicked in.

Before he could breathe a word to me, I marched right up to him and slammed my palms down on his desk. Papers scattered and a jar of pens hit the floor.

"Why the hell didn't you tell me about the other missing children?" I screamed, smacking my hands down on the table half a dozen times.

"Whoa!" he said, standing up and holding out his hands defensively. "What is this about, Miss von Derbach?" he asked, looking strangely afraid of me despite his gun and badge.

"It's *Doctor* von Derbach," I corrected him. I'd been dying to point that out to someone all week.

*Who better to do it to than this jackass?*

"Sorry," he muttered, adjusting his gun belt uncomfortably. "To answer your question, Doctor...every few years we do have a drowning around these parts and lots of them is kids, which is to be expected. None of those kids were reported missing. They were all on or near the water when they fell in. Like we explained to you before, this lake empties into the Meade River, making it nearly impossible to locate lost bodies."

"I want the names of those children," I demanded, placing my hands on my hips sternly. "And their parents!"

I expected him to put up a fuss, but he simply said, "Okay." I sat in a metal chair by the entrance while he took his time writing down names. I wasn't sure where I was going with this, but it had to be somewhere. I had to know what happened to my son that day at the lake, once and for all.

133

# CHAPTER THIRTY-ONE

"I even added the years they died with a description, and I put them in order of the years they died for you," Sheriff Baggins said, thrusting the list at me. He looked pleased with himself.

"Thanks." I stuffed it into my purse and turned to leave.

"I think it would be a great idea for you to hook up with the other parents of those lost children. You guys could really help support each other," he said, smiling.

I wrinkled up my nose at him. I remembered my advice to Bart, about getting together with Robert Tuttle, and I wondered if he felt the same way I did when I heard it. *Just because we've lost kids doesn't mean we're all friends, or the same.*

I drove to my campsite, but along the way, I stopped at a local camp store to pick up some firewood and lighter fluid. I knew I would need it tonight if I planned on sitting outside. Right now I

134

just wanted to get back to the camper and study that list.

\*\*\*

The first reported drowning was a boy named Tommy Mitchell in the summer of 1999. He was sixteen years old when he disappeared from where he was swimming with his three cousins. He was there one minute and gone the next.

The second one took place in the summer of 2001. A thirteen-year-old girl named Mandy was riding on the back of her father's jet ski with an older friend when she fell off and never resurfaced. Another child at Lake Merlott—another tragedy.

In 2003, another thirteen year old named Cynthia Thomas fell off her family's sailboat similarly to Sully.

In 2005, two local brothers, ages fourteen and fifteen—Rex and Albert Shaw—went swimming during a thunderstorm. They never returned home.

In 2007, a seventeen-year-old named Isabel Morrison was riding on a tube behind her family's boat when she disappeared underwater. Like all of the others, her body never surfaced.

And finally, in 2009, it was my son's turn. No kids had drowned or disappeared at the lake since Sully—he was the last one, according to this list.

My hands shook ceaselessly, but I gripped the paper tight. I couldn't stand to look at the names or descriptions, but I couldn't look away, either. Was it just a coincidence that for the past fifteen years a child went missing from the lake? *Kids drown. It happens all the time. Every day in this country...*

*But what about the bodies? They vanished completely.*

I picked up the picture of Sully and examined it more carefully. The boy in the picture was pale and faded, but his body wasn't transparent—he wasn't floating or doing anything else to confirm he was a ghost.

I didn't want to think it, but I couldn't help myself. *Was it possible...could my son still be alive?*

# CHAPTER THIRTY-TWO

For the second time today, I knocked on Aubrey Chetfield's door. If she was surprised to see me, she didn't show it.

"I talked to Sheriff Baggins. I believe you and I need some help."

She opened up the door, and I followed her to a small dinette table. It was one of those tables that can seat six, but she had it folded down for two.

"Are you married?" I asked, feeling rude for not asking earlier.

"No," she said simply. A plate filled with chips and a fresh turkey sandwich was sitting on the table. I'd obviously interrupted her dinner hour.

"Please finish your meal first," I said apologetically.

"It's all right. I never get much of an appetite anymore, anyway," she said, waving her hand at the plate. "Going through the motions...but you already know what that's like, don't you?"

I took a seat at the table beside her. I pushed the list toward her. "Can you give me more information about any of these cases? Also, are any of these families local, besides Rex and Albert Shaw?" I asked. No reason to beat around the bush.

"Besides the details listed here, the only thing I know is that all of the children were slightly troubled," she said softly.

"What teenager isn't?" I asked bitterly, immediately recognizing the defensive tone in my voice. "Sorry," I said, staring down at the list until Sheriff Baggins' unexpectedly neat handwriting became a blur.

Sully was troubled before the incident. *But what did that really matter?*

"And as far as your next question, the answer is yes. Three of the children on that list were local. The two brothers, Rex and Albert, were from this community. Their father lives on the other side of the lake," she said, tapping at their names on the list. She was quiet for a moment, deep in thought. "You said three children. Who was the third child?"

Silently, she pointed at Isabel's name.

"Where do her parents live?" I prompted her.

She cleared her throat. "Isabel was my daughter," she said, running her fingers back and forth over the dead girl's name.

# CHAPTER THIRTY-THREE

I stared at her daughter's name on the list. *Isabel Morrison.*

"I don't understand. Her last name is different from yours," I said, searching her eyes questioningly.

"Morrison was my married name and Izzy's father's surname. He left shortly after she went missing. He couldn't handle it anymore. The pain of her loss, that is…you see, we weren't from around here. I bought this place…after Izzy…he hated me for never wanting to leave this place, the place where our daughter died."

I nodded sympathetically. "Were you with her when it happened?" I asked tentatively. She nodded again.

"She was on the tube when I looked back. I even took a few quick snapshots of her. The last time I looked at her, she gave me this weird little wave. I like to imagine that in her own little way, she was telling me goodbye.

"When I looked back for the last and final time, she was gone. I wasn't overly concerned. I thought she'd simply fallen off the raft. Her father turned the boat around to fetch her, but she wasn't back there. At first, we thought she was playing a prank. But after several minutes passed, we drove back the direction we came from, and scanned the waters, thinking perhaps she'd fallen off earlier and we had stopped too late. We drove every inch of that entire lake and contacted the authorities. Like you, our child was never found. You know that moment—when you realize someone or something important is missing? That feeling of dread in your chest? Well, that's what I felt that day—only it never ever went away."

"I'm so sorry," I said, unsure of anything else to say. Now I knew what everyone else felt like, trying to think of what to say to me or how to act around me after Sully died. I didn't know what to say to this woman.

"They never found her body?" I asked, although I already knew the answer.

She shook her head. "When they analyzed the rope, they found traces of blood. They speculated that she hit her head on a piece of driftwood and sunk like a rock. Then her body washed downstream and out to the river."

I nearly stopped breathing as I listened to her recall the details of her daughter's supposed death. The grisly details sounded eerily familiar to my own tragedy. "They found Sully's blood on the side of the boat," I said flatly.

"I know. They found traces of blood in all of the cases except Rex and Albert. There was no trace of them at all, but everyone assumed they drowned, since they'd last been seen in the water," she told me.

"What about the other boys who were just swimming when they disappeared?" I asked.

"They found blood on nearby rocks in those cases. In nearly all of the cases, the speculations were that they hit their head on something and then drowned. But let me ask you a question. If they drew blood and they went unconscious, wouldn't you expect to find more blood? I would expect a pool of blood to float on the surface of the water, leading us straight to the bodies. Furthermore, we all started searching the water immediately. None of us found our children. Could a body really float downriver that quickly, as frantically as we searched?"

Her words felt like daggers, penetrating my invisible cloak of denial. I wanted her to stop talking, but she pushed on anyway.

"Did you know that most bodies float? The fatter you are, the more likely it is that you will surface, and the Shaw boys were both obese. It doesn't make sense. You have to admit it—*it doesn't make sense.*"

Her arguments were compelling. "But what are you suggesting by all this, Aubrey? That our children are alive and well? That their deaths were just a hoax?"

My questions were not in anger; I truly wanted to understand…

My mind was gargled, thoughts spinning out of control…

"No. I believe that they are all dead," she said.

"Then why do the details matter?" I demanded.

"Because I believe that someone murdered those children. *Our* children."

# CHAPTER THIRTY-FOUR

"What you're say...is i-impossible!" I stammered, shoving my chair back so I could get up and leave. "So, what do you think happened? Someone waited underwater to snatch our children? When they grabbed them, they were then able to drag them all the way to shore and away from here without anyone seeing them? Like some sort of underwater boogeyman?" I cried, leaning toward her, my face inches from hers.

But she sat there, not answering, staring at the uneaten sandwich.

"That is ludicrous!" I sat back down in the chair, exasperated.

The thought of my son drowning was hard enough. I didn't need some crazy lady telling me that someone murdered him!

"Maybe it wasn't a person. Maybe it was a demon or an evil spirit," Aubrey quietly spoke, laying her hands flat on the table in front of her.

143

"Now you're saying that they were killed by underwater demons?" I scoffed.

"I thought you believed in otherworldly beings?" she asked, narrowing her eyes at me suspiciously.

"Just because I follow stupid ghost stories doesn't mean I actually believe in them," I replied calmly.

"So, in other words, you are a *dis*believer. People call on you for help when they are haunted by ghosts. If they knew the truth about you and your skepticism, do you think they would really call on you? Not in a million years," she spat. I wanted to say something, defend myself. But something about her words rang true.

*Maybe the best thing for me to do is get the hell out of this town and abandon this entire profession...*

# CHAPTER THIRTY-FIVE

The fire crackled and spit tiny, little pieces of flames in my direction. I was holding a hotdog on a stick and I'd extended it out into the fire. It was perfectly black on every side but I just kept cooking it anyway, rolling it back and forth in a mind numbing task.

I couldn't get Aubrey's words out of my head. *Was she right?* I wasn't sure.

Part of being objective was following the scientific evidence and observing what could be explained, not following *feelings*, or believing in mythical creatures.

At least that's what I thought. But maybe being objective in my line of work should also include not ruling out the premise that ghosts may exist.

Perhaps I was so set on *not* finding any, that I'd become completely biased in the other direction. I didn't want to be a believer, but I also didn't want to be a critic. I needed to bring more fairness to my investigations.

I was going to solve this case, one way or another. *Like I said earlier, I'm no quitter.*

I pulled the wiener out of the fire and slid it onto a bun. It was way too burnt for my liking, but I chewed it anyway, not tasting a bit of it.

I thought about when Sully was five and we camped for the first time in our backyard. I built a fire for us and laid out sleeping bags on the grass. We cooked hotdogs and s'mores, and then we told stories as we lay on our backs staring up at the stars. He was so happy and so easy to please at that age. *I thought it was hard—dealing with a small child. But those were the easy days, when I could still trick him into loving me...*

My plan for tomorrow was to visit the Shaw residence and try to reach some of the other deceased kids' parents via phone. Close to nightfall, I planned to set up shop in the woods behind Aubrey's house with my video camera. I was going to monitor the entire woods, no matter how long it took, until I either saw my son's ghost or found an explanation for the picture she captured.

The picture...I pulled it out of my jean shorts pocket, staring at his face again. It seemed legit and Aubrey had no reason to lie.

*But I suppose I really need to have it examined by an expert to make sure it's not a fake.*

I pulled my cell phone out of my pocket. I had several missed calls from Dr. Paddison. I knew she was concerned and checking up on me, but I wasn't in the mood for lectures. Or pep talks.

# CHAPTER THIRTY-SIX

"Whatever you're selling, I ain't buying!" yelled a gruff male voice from the other side of the door of the Shaws' house.

"I'm not selling anything, Mr. Shaw. I'm here to talk to you about your sons," I called through the door, feeling uneasy.

The door sprung open. A middle-aged mountain of a man stood in the doorway.

"What do you want to know about those two no-good sons of bitches?" he roared. I took a step back. The look in his eyes was wild, and he smelled like a mixture of body odor, alcohol, and tobacco.

"I'm sorry to disturb you, sir. If I'm not mistaken, your sons are deceased, is that right?"

"Uh huh. That's right."

"But you just called them…"

"No-good sons of bitches," he finished, repeating himself for me.

"Pardon me for saying this, but why speak ill of

the dead? Especially your dead *children*?" I asked, anger rising in my chest.

"Because those two dumb asses wandered off from their chores to go swimming, and they went and let themselves drown. Now what the hell do you need?" he boomed.

My best bet was to turn around and leave, but I continued on anyway.

"My son died in the lake too. I heard a report that his ghost was sighted here," I said boldly, unknowingly puffing out my chest.

He roared with laughter. Then he did the unthinkable—as though laughing in my face wasn't enough—he slammed the door on me.

*What an asshole!* I thought bitterly. I turned on my heels and got the hell out of there.

\*\*\*

I searched online for some of the other parents. I was able to track down contact numbers for three of them. All three were a dead end. One was a wrong number, another was disconnected, and I received no answer or voicemail on the third one. By the end of the day, I felt slightly defeated.

But I kept going. I decided that if I could handle one door in my face, then I could take a few more. There were several other lake homes spread out on both sides of the lake. Perhaps someone else had seen Sully's ghost besides Aubrey. It was time to go door to door.

# CHAPTER THIRTY-SEVEN

I started with Aubrey's closest neighbor. They were 'The Tanners,' according to their mailbox. *I will never understand why people put up signs announcing who they are on the outside of their homes.*

A handsome, dark-haired woman came to the door when I rang the bell. I have to admit that I felt slightly foolish, but what did I have to lose at this point? I told her my name and held up the picture. "Have you seen this boy around here?" I asked, getting straight to the point.

I decided at the last minute not to use the word 'ghost' unless someone else brought it up first.

"No, can't say that I have. I live in New York for nine months out of the year, and this place is just a summer hideaway. I just got in on Tuesday morning," she said, with an unmistakable New York accent.

"Thank you," I said, backing up from her

149

doorway.

The next house I approached was a small cottage, tucked away in a heavily shaded area close to the lake. There will neat little stones lining the narrow pathway leading to the front door.

A plump, elderly woman answered my knock. I repeated the same spiel.

"No, I haven't seen anyone who looks like him lately. But he does look familiar…"

I knew what was coming next.

"Isn't that the dead boy? One of those kids who drowned in the lake? Yes. Yes, I remember him now from the news," she said, nodding at the picture adamantly.

She looked up at me strangely, studying my face. "You're his mother, aren't you?"

"Yes," I admitted. And then, "One of your neighbors reported seeing him. She snapped this photo of him." I held up the strange, faded image of a boy that looked like my son.

"Which neighbor?" she asked suspiciously. I couldn't see a way around the truth, so I told her it was Aubrey Chetfield.

"I see," she said, tapping a finger on her chin thoughtfully. "Would you like to come in? I have cookies," she offered. I accepted her invitation.

I sat down on a plastic-covered sofa and selected an oatmeal raisin cookie from a tin platter on the glass coffee table in front of me. My belly was rumbling; I'd skipped out on breakfast this morning, which wasn't a great idea. I can always tell when my blood sugar is low because I always get shaky and weak. I ate the cookie and then picked up another one.

"These are the best oatmeal raisin cookies I've ever had," I complimented her.

"Thank you, dear," she said, sitting down beside me and taking her own cookie.

She still held Sully's picture in her hand. She chewed her cookie, staring at it again. Finally, she handed it back to me.

"Aubrey is a little unstable. She has been, and understandably so, since her daughter passed away. I've lived here my entire life and I've never seen any ghosts."

"How do you explain the photo then?" I asked, munching the cookie slowly.

She shrugged. "I can't tell you that. But I do know that Aubrey's been hospitalized several times for severe depression. She's even tried to commit suicide a few times." I stopped munching.

I thought about Aubrey all alone in that house, with her daughter dead in the lake and her husband long gone...

I knew what it was like to deal with tragedy, but I'd never considered suicide.

"That's terrible," I said, not sure how to respond.

"So, she's not the most reliable source of information. Calling you in Indiana and giving you hope that your son is alive..." She shook her head from side to side, disapproving.

"My name is Marlene, by the way. My husband, Rick, is whittling wood in the basement," she explained.

"Well, thank you for your time and the cookies," I said, brushing the crumbs from my lap. I stood up to leave, feeling tired and disappointed.

"The two houses to the left of me are vacant. Don't want you to waste your time, dear. I'm so sorry about your loss," she said sincerely.

I skipped the next two houses, and was once again on the other side of the lake near the Shaw house. The next two houses I approached appeared to be occupied, but I got no answer when I knocked. *People around here probably spend a lot of time boating. That's probably where they are.*

It didn't seem as though I was getting much accomplished, and my feet were beginning to ache. I still had hours before nightfall. I decided maybe it was time to get that photo looked at by an expert.

# CHAPTER THIRTY-EIGHT

In the movies, there's always some fancy crime lab you can visit, where an expert photo examiner can take a gander at the picture in question. That is not the case in this lake town, or any other town I've visited in my life. I've had to inspect photos in the past, and I've always found that the best source for examining them are professional photographers themselves.

I got busy with the task of tracking one down online that was both professional and close in proximity. After doing a little research, I was shocked to discover that one of the residents of Lake Merlott actually had a website, identifying himself as a professional photographer for hire. His name was Mason Kincaid and the address to his "studio" actually belonged to one of the houses on the other side of the lake that I'd attempted to visit today.

No one answered his door, but the website

included an email address and telephone number. I opted to try both avenues for contacting him.

It was Sunday, which meant my chances of getting someone to talk to me were slim, but it was worth a shot anyway. I first sent an email describing my location and requesting assistance with photo evaluation. Then I called. No answer. I was tempted to march over there and knock again, but I decided that was too hasty, and I'd have a better shot of retaining his services if I waited patiently.

It didn't take long. As I was chopping up lettuce for a Caesar salad, I heard the ding of a new email. I finished chopping and added some dressing before sitting back down in front of the computer. The email read,

    "I'm home. Please come now."

I jumped up, abandoning my lunch. I slipped on a pair of flip-flops and jogged to the other side of the lake, ignoring the pain in my feet.

The one-story small framed house that had once been shrouded in darkness was brightened with porch lights and a twinkling, awe inspiring chandelier that shined from a large bay window.

Mason Kincaid was standing at the door waiting for me. He looked to be around thirty, with a partially shaved head and lanky build.

"Hello, there!" he greeted me, waving enthusiastically.

"Hi! Thank you so much for agreeing to see me on a Sunday, Mr. Kincaid. I truly appreciate it."

"Please call me Mason," he said, allowing me

inside the modern, spotless foyer of his small, but trendy, home.

The foyer opened up into a small living room filled with oddly designed, eclectic furniture. His walls were covered with paintings that resembled the splattered masterpieces of Jackson Pollock. "Your work?" I inquired, pointing up at one of the colorful pieces. He nodded, looking mildly embarrassed.

"And these also?" I asked, pointing at a cluster of black and white photographs of Lake Merlott.

"Yes. Artwork and photography are my passions, but right now they don't pay the bills. Believe it or not, my day job is working on an assembly line at a machine shop in town." I raised my eyebrows.

"I do find that a little hard to believe. You're very talented," I said, trying to be polite.

"Would you like something to drink? Coffee, tea, or soda?"

"Tea sounds great," I said, surprised by how comfortable I felt around this young stranger. He wasn't much younger than me and he was attractive, but this wasn't the time for romance...

I followed Mason to a compact kitchen with modern appliances and smooth wooden flooring. "Your house may be one of the smallest on the lake, but it's by far the neatest and most intriguing I've seen," I told him genuinely. He poured two icy glasses of tea.

"Thank you! Some of the houses up here are outrageous in price, but I found this surprisingly affordable," he explained.

"Why did you choose to live here? At Lake

Merlott, I mean?"

"Besides the fact that it's an inspiring location for my artwork, this place holds very fond memories for me. I spent a lot of time here as a kid."

"Me too," I said, taking a sip of my tea. "I only wish I could say the same about having fond memories."

"You have bad memories of this place? How come?" he asked, sitting down at a green, blob-shaped table in the corner of the room. I sat down in a seat close to him. His legs were long and the table was small, so our knees were practically touching.

"My son drowned in this lake five years ago." I put it out there, ripping the Band-Aid off. He froze mid-sip.

"How old was your son?" he asked.

"Thirteen at the time. I had him young," I explained, reading his mind. "One of your neighbors, Aubrey Chetfield, sent me this photo," I said, pulling the photo in question out of my bag.

I slid it over to him to examine. "Can you tell me if the picture has been doctored in any way?" I asked.

"I can try," he said with a look of pure determination.

# CHAPTER THIRTY-NINE

After uploading the picture to his computer, Mason set to work examining the photo for authenticity. He was quiet and methodical as he worked. He finally looked up from the computer and said, "There are many different ways to determine if a photo has been doctored or not. With technology today, people can do almost anything when it comes to altering photography. They do it all the time, putting phony videos on YouTube and doctored photos on their Facebook accounts." I nodded, listening intently.

"How can you tell exactly?" I was interested for a variety of reasons; one reason being that I'd like to be able to examine future photos on my own. But mostly because I needed to know if this could possibly be my son.

"As I'm sure you know, most ghostly anomalies can be explained by dust particles, insects, or photo processing errors. That's not possible in this case because the image in the photo is a clear cut image of a figure, specifically your son. Doctoring a photo is a whole different issue. First, I always examine the megapixels to see if they've been altered. I also examine the image itself for discrepancies in the size, surrounding shadows, or geometric patterns. Let me ask you this: is it possible that someone could have obtained a photo of your son online, and then cropped it and pasted it into a woodsy background?" he asked, eyeing me intently.

"I've never seen a photo like this before in my life. It's not a replica of any of my personal photographs of Sully." He nodded, moving back to examine the photograph.

Finally, he leaned back in the computer chair lazily. "This picture does not appear to be doctored or altered in any way. It seems legitimate. With that being said, there's someone you need to talk to," he said, looking at me gravely.

"Who?" I asked, unsure where this conversation was headed.

"My neighbor, Cici Gray. Last year, she claimed she saw a ghost too." I nearly fainted right there in my seat.

# CHAPTER FORTY

I followed Mason a short couple of meters to the cabin of Cici Gray. I'd been here merely an hour before, and I'd had no luck with knocking or the doorbell. But as soon as Mason rapped on the door, it flew open.

"Oh, my! My long lost neighbor! You're right next door and I haven't seen you in nearly a month," she complained ruefully, shaking a long, crooked finger at Mason.

Cici Gray looked close to a hundred years old, with short, thinning, bluish-white hair. She was frail like a bird and stood with a considerable hunch in her back. Her eyes moved to me next.

"I saw you through the blinds earlier, young lady. But I don't answer the door to strangers," she answered firmly.

"I understand completely," I said, offering a forgiving smile.

"Look at me! Standing here jabbering instead of inviting you guys inside." We followed her into an old-fashioned family room cluttered with antiques and musty, old books. She offered us coffee but we both declined.

I wasn't in the mood for niceties; I needed to know if the ghost Cici claimed she saw was my son. I handed her the photo and waited for a reaction. Her eyebrows furrowed, and she looked from me to Mason with a puzzled expression. "So, you've seen him too," she whispered.

# CHAPTER FORTY-ONE

According to Cici Gray, she'd seen Sully in the woods behind her house on three different occasions in the past five years, most of them recent. "I knew he was dead. I recognized his face from the paper and TV news," she explained.

"Did he speak?" I asked, scooting to the edge of my seat. My heart was beating a million times per minute, my shoulders shaking uncontrollably.

"No. Each time, it was pitch black dark outside and I spotted a figure deep in the woods from my back porch. As I moved closer, I saw his face. I shouted to him, but then he was gone. He vanished."

"But how do you know it was a ghost? Could he have been real? We never found his body in the lake that day. Perhaps he just ran away from you because he was spooked for some reason?" I asked, my voice rising in excitement and fear.

"No. He was dead. He vanished. There were no

161

sounds of him walking in the woods. He didn't take off in a sprint. He didn't duck behind a tree. He was there one minute and gone the next."

I was baffled. Two people reporting the same ghost? Was this possible? My evidence meter was blinking.

"Do you know Aubrey Chetfield?" I asked, suddenly wondering if they were conspiring together. Although for what reason, I had no idea. I tried to silence the skeptic inside of me. I couldn't see what either of the women had to gain from playing a trick on me. Neither of them even knew me before this week.

"Yes, I've seen Aubrey around the lake a couple times, but we've never spoken," she said.

I nodded, mulling over the details. "I know that you told Mason about the ghost, but why didn't you call the police? Didn't you find it odd, seeing a dead boy behind your house?" I asked quizzically.

"I would have thought it was strange, but this wasn't the first time, my dear. Over the past several years, I've seen a few of the others in that same area of the woods," she admitted quietly.

\*\*\*

I thanked her and Mason for their time and help, and I took off out the door. I had to talk to Aubrey again and get my camera equipment set up before nightfall. I was walking at a rapid pace, sucking in the smells of pine when I heard a distinct crunching sound behind me in the woods. I froze.

"It's just me," Mason called out, jogging to catch

up with me. "I'm coming with you," he said, finally reaching my side.

"I work alone," I said firmly, still moving.

"Please let me help," he said, stepping right in front of me so that he was only a few inches from my face. "Please. I feel this overwhelming need to protect you."

I didn't know what to say to that. I stood there looking at him, dumbfounded.

The next thing I knew, he was placing his lips on mine. This couldn't have come at a worse time in my life, but I didn't pull away. I let him slip his tongue inside of my mouth and I gripped his shoulders. This was turning out to be the strangest case I'd ever worked.

# CHAPTER FORTY-TWO

When Aubrey Chetfield opened the door for us, she was wearing her usual somber expression. "Hello, Mr. Kincaid," she said, nodding at her neighbor cordially. I let myself in, Mason following behind me.

"I had Mason review the photo you took of Sully. He's a professional photographer, knows a lot about photos and manipulation..." I was talking so fast, my tongue was sticking to the roof of my mouth. "Well, he confirmed that the photo hasn't been doctored."

"I knew that already. I'm the one who took the photograph, remember?" she said sarcastically.

"I'm sorry, Aubrey. I just had to be certain. One of your other neighbors, Cici Gray, has also seen Sully," I told her excitedly.

She raised her eyebrows in an atypical display of emotion.

"She also claims that she saw some of the other

164

missing kids."

"My Izzy?" she asked breathlessly.

"I'm not certain. She did describe a teenage girl, but the only way to know for sure is to show her a picture," I explained.

"I'll go see her now," Aubrey announced, standing up from her chair and rummaging in one of her cabinets for a photo of Isabel.

"Before you go, may I ask you one question about the night you saw Sully?" She was distracted now, piling up a stack of snapshots on the coffee table to take to Cici.

"Uh huh," she said, never taking her eyes away from the photos.

"How did you know Sully was a ghost, and not real?"

"Because I didn't hear him running away. He was just gone," she murmured. I know I only said one question, but I had to ask one more. "If it was dark outside, how did you take the photo of my son?"

"I just turned the flash on, silly," she said with a snort.

Aubrey was Miss Personality today.

I bid her goodbye, and headed back to my campsite with Mason in tow, so that I could ponder over the day's events. My thoughts solely revolved around my son, and the possibility that he could still be alive.

# CHAPTER FORTY-THREE

I'd planned on keeping my scheme to investigate the woods a secret from Mason. But that plan went flying out the window when he asked me directly, "You're going out there tonight, aren't you?"

I'd only just met him, but somehow I sensed he could see straight through my façade.

"I am," I admitted with a sigh. He followed me inside the cramped RV. *It felt strange, having someone inside it with me again.*

"And I must insist that you let me do this alone."

He started to protest, but I held my hand up to stop him. "Save it," I said seriously. "If there's a possibility that my son, ghost or not, is out in these woods, I will not let your presence scare him off. Everyone who has seen him has been in the dark and alone. I'm trying to recreate the scene by placing myself in the dark by myself, just like Aubrey and Cici were when they experienced their sightings."

He pursed his lips and pinched the bridge of his nose. "You won't change your mind, will you?" he asked.

"Not a chance," I said, relishing in his concern for me. It had been so long since any man had expressed an interest in me, and I must admit I was enthralled by it.

I had zero appetite, but I was eager to be hospitable. I finally decided on a frozen pizza and I slid it into the oven.

*What I wouldn't give right now for one of Bart's home cooked meals!* I thought, remembering the fancy pasta we'd shared.

Mason and I ate our pizza in silence. He finally broke it by saying, "Please let me do one thing for you." I didn't like the sound of this, but I decided to hear him out.

"I have a lot of expensive video equipment. Please let me lend it to you for your investigation. Tell me where you want the cameras and how many, and I will hide them in the trees for you. After I'm done, I will go home and leave you to do your investigation in peace. Scout's honor." "You got a deal," I said, smiling at him gratefully.

# CHAPTER
# FORTY-FOUR

Mason worked methodically, attaching tiny cameras to the wooded areas behind both Aubrey and Cici's properties, with their permission, of course. I watched him, admiringly.

"I can't tell you enough how much I appreciate this. The amount of video cameras you own is freaking crazy!" I said, following him to the final tree, where he attached the last camera.

"There are thirteen of them total. If you don't find what you're looking for in these areas, we can move them around tomorrow night."

"Thank you," I said, draping my arms around him and giving him a tremendous hug. I didn't know what was going on between us exactly, but I liked it. It all seemed too sudden and too fast, but maybe that's how some of the best relationships are formed. I wouldn't know. Besides the two month relationship I had with Sully's biological father, I'd never had any true, meaningful relationships with a man.

Besides my son, of course. He was the first and last love of my life.

"You have your cell phone?" Mason asked for the millionth time.

"Yes. And a flashlight too. I'll call you if I have any trouble. And I won't fall in the lake," I coaxed him. "Now get out of here!" I playfully shoved him away.

"Okay. I don't want to go, but I will," he said, sighing and rubbing his hands.

He eventually became a shape in the distance, and then he disappeared altogether. It was time to get to work. The sun was slowly fading beyond the horizon, and I watched it disappear completely. I had a flashlight but I planned on using it sparingly and only when necessary.

If I wanted to recreate the scene, then I had to hang out in the dark. Instead of sitting in a chair like I did at Bart's, tonight I was opting to stay on foot.

I was starting out tonight's adventure directly behind Aubrey's lake house, and then I planned to eventually take a stroll to the other side near Cici's cabin, where the second sighting occurred.

Aubrey was aware of my presence out here, and I got the feeling that she was watching me from the window. I couldn't say that I blamed her. She now had a stake in all of this, now that her deceased daughter had possibly been spotted as well.

The lake was up ahead, still and calm, its surface sparkling like tiny little jewels in the moonlight. Again, I was struck with the strange notion that a place so beautiful should not have such an ugly history.

I could still feel Aubrey's invisible eyes on me, so I ventured down closer to the shore, and hopefully, out of her sight. I took a seat down near the water. I stared into its murky darkness, daring it to challenge me in some way. *Take me instead*, I dared its ugly waters.

As I looked across the lake, I could see more woods and the twinkle of house lights in the distance. I wondered if Mason was somewhere out there watching too. I stayed there, silent, for nearly an hour. I listened and watched for any suspicious sights or sounds. There was nothing out of the ordinary.

It was time to walk. I took my time, silently hoping to be confronted by a ghost, preferably my son's. When I reached a halfway point between Aubrey and Cici's houses, I took a seat on the dry, earthy ground. I was wearing old jeans and a Nike sweatshirt, so I wasn't concerned about getting a little dirty.

After spending the better half of an hour sitting in that place, I decided to move again. I crept slowly along the shoreline, where the lake curved and the houses on the other side began. As I walked downhill, my foot hit the side of a tree root and I fell to the ground on my knee.

My knee hit the tip of a sharp rock, and I let out a small howl of pain.

*What a dummy*, I chastised myself, standing back up and wiping the dirt from my jeans.

As I straightened up and began walking forward, I saw the unmistakable shape of a person just several feet ahead of me. I squinted into the darkness, trying to sharpen my focus. Whoever it was, they were walking toward me, and *fast*.

*Was Mason back? Or was it the ghost of one of the missing children?*

As soon as my eyes adjusted, it was too late. A man in a slick, black leather mask was headed straight for me. There was something in his hand. *A gun?* I wondered. I let out a scream and turned on my heels to run. But that's when I felt something heavy slam into the back of my head. I hit the ground with a loud "oomph" and then my whole world turned to black.

# CHAPTER FORTY-FIVE

When I opened my eyes, I had no idea where I was. All I could see was blackness. My head felt heavy, my thoughts fuzzy.

*What the hell happened to me?* But then it all came rushing back.

The horrifying man in the mask. He was walking toward me with a metal bat in his hand. *I tried to run...but he got me*, I remembered hastily.

I was lying on my side in the darkness. I forced myself to lift up to a sitting position. Neither my hands nor feet were tied, thank goodness.

I immediately started feeling around in the darkness. I knew one thing for sure: I wasn't outside anymore.

There were walls on all sides of me. What was this, a tiny room? *A closet*, some rational voice inside my head informed me. I froze.

How long had I been in here? Was I going to suffocate? I tried to fight off the rising panic in my chest, but it was becoming harder and harder to breathe.

*Get a handle on yourself, Veronica.* I counted backwards from fifty, and took several slow, long breaths.

When I opened my eyes, they started to adjust in the darkness. I was, in fact, in a closet. The door was constructed of heavy wood, the walls on both sides of me made of plaster. A stiff metal rod lined with hangers holding clothes hung above my head. I was surrounded by the fragrance of musty old clothing and dust.

I had to get out of here.

A tarnished, brass knob was the only thing keeping me in here, but I knew it couldn't be that easy…I turned it slowly.

Unsurprisingly, I was locked in tight. *I'm trapped in here*, I realized. But where is *here*?

I suddenly remembered the flashlight in my pocket. And speaking of pockets, my cell phone!

I dug frantically through my pockets, pulling out both.

I turned the phone on. No service, big shocker. I pulled myself up to a crouching position and moved the phone around, trying to find at least a glimmer of a signal. No such luck.

The phone was a source of light, but the flashlight was brighter. I flipped it on, my fingers trembling.

I held the phone out in front of me, and with trembling fingers, I sent a text to everyone I knew: my dad, Judy, Margaret, Dr. Paddison, and Mason. I instantly received error messages in return, informing me that my messages failed to be delivered.

*Well, at least I tried*, I thought dejectedly. *I have to do something.*

I fought the urge to scream. If my attacker was somewhere in this house, I didn't want to alert him to my state of consciousness. The last thing I needed was another blow to the head. *The next one might be fatal.*

I shone the light around, trying to get a sense of my surroundings. The clothes were moth eaten and possibly decades old. I started digging through jacket and pants pockets, looking for a key, or at least a bobby pin. I'd never picked a lock before, but there's a first time for everything, right?

I found a few random scraps of paper and a disgusting old handkerchief in the pockets. I shoved the clothes aside, looking for some sort of trap door or something I could use in the back of the closet. There was simply more plaster.

I felt around on the floor, shining my light around the entire contours of the space. There was a small step stool and three cardboard boxes with shoes.

I was about to resort to kicking and screaming at the door when I saw the outline of a small square door in the ceiling of the closet. *It must be some sort of attic space!*

I wasn't sure if I could wrench the small wooden door open, but I had to give it a shot. I piled up the shoe boxes on the stepping stool. It wasn't a safe method of climbing, but I'd take a broken ankle over death by suffocation—or death by a crazed

174

killer—any day of the week.

I climbed on the top box, but the opening was still too far. I was going to have to pull myself up onto the clothing rod and stand on top of it.

The rod resembled metal, and I could only pray that it would hold my weight.

*This is my only chance of survival.*

# CHAPTER FORTY-SIX

When I was in high school, I nearly failed Phys Ed because I could never do a pull-up. My upper body has always been petite compared to my curvy bottom, and lifting my lower half is a daunting task.

I was worried I couldn't do it—pull myself up onto this rod—but adrenaline is a funny thing. When it's surging through your body in a life or death situation, it can make you capable of anything.

I lifted myself up, stood on the bar, and slammed my fists into the small trapdoor in the ceiling. It gave way easily.

The open hole revealed more darkness beyond, but I placed my hands on the sides of the tiny space and I pulled myself up through it.

I collapsed onto a dark, wooden floor. I was in an attic of some kind.

Out of breath, all I wanted to do was lie there on the cold, bare floor and suck in deep cool breaths.

But I couldn't take the risk, and I wasn't home free yet. At any moment, my captor could discover my whereabouts. *I need to go somewhere from here, but where? How?*

My ascent into the attic wasn't a quiet affair, and he could be on his way to kill me *right now* for all I knew...

I dug the flashlight out again and shone it around the dark space. The ceiling was very low and the floor was covered in boxes. I saw a light up ahead, so I army crawled through the dusty space, and was shocked to discover a small window. The light came courtesy of the moon.

As I looked through the window, I realized where I was. I was in the attic of one of the vacant lake houses. Someone had put me here.

I couldn't go back down to the closet, and I didn't see any other openings in the floor. The window held the key to my freedom.

As I looked down below, I saw a wooden canopy two floors below. The canopy was probably the covering for the porch. I had no choice. I had to jump.

Without a second thought, I slid the window open and I scooted my body out onto a tiny, narrow ledge. The canopy below was my closest destination. I wouldn't die from this height, but if I landed wrong I could sustain serious injuries.

I said a silent prayer and leapt off the ledge feet first.

# CHAPTER FORTY-SEVEN

My feet hit the hard surface of the canopy with a thud. But then I went rolling, and the next thing I knew, I was hanging off the very edge. The only thing that saved me from hitting the ground was the hood of my sweatshirt.

I was hanging from a raggedy edge, and I had to get down from here. The ground wasn't that far, at least that's what I told myself.

I started swinging my legs wildly, rocking back and forth. I finally heard a loud rip and I toppled to the ground, banging up my knees and elbows.

I felt sharp pain surging through every part of my body, but I jumped up and ran away as fast as I could, ignoring the roaring pain.

Mason's house was only a few houses away, and I prayed like hell I could make it after all of the obstacles I'd overcome thus far. His porch light shone like a heavenly beacon in the distance up ahead.

I pounded the ground with my Nikes until I eventually reached the front door. I tried the knob but it was locked. I started banging on it frantically. It seemed like an eternity before the door opened.

Mason stood there in the doorframe, like an angel sent from above. I fell into his arms, and then I promptly passed out again.

# CHAPTER
# FORTY-EIGHT

I woke up in a starched white hospital room. The first thing I saw when I opened my eyes was Mason by my side. His eyes were red-rimmed and his face was creased with worry. "We have to call the police," I said, in a gravelly, strained voice that I barely recognized as my own.

"Sheriff Baggins has already come and gone. According to him, if whoever did this to you had wanted to kill you, they would have. He had some problems with a couple of rowdy teenage boys at the campground last night, and he suspects it was one of them playing a cruel prank on you."

I closed my eyes in horror. "This was no prank. My attacker hit me over the head with a metal bat and left me to die in a closet." I told him the entire story.

"I'm calling Sheriff Baggins and I'm telling his ass to get down here to take your statement," he said angrily. He bent over and kissed me on the cheek before walking out into the hallway with his cell phone.

"Mason, wait. Don't bother calling him. We might be able to identify the culprit ourselves," I called out to him.

"How?" he asked, turning to look at me as though I was crazy.

"The cameras," I croaked. My throat was *really* hurting now; it felt like I'd swallowed a knife. Or ten knives, more like it.

"I have a pretty good idea of what happened to the cameras. My guess is that your attacker destroyed them."

"Maybe not all of them," I said, hopefully.

"I hope you're right," he said, scratching his head in thought. "Maybe we can see his face," he remarked thoughtfully.

"He was wearing a mask. But maybe there will be something else we can use to identify him," I explained. His face fell with the mention of the word *mask*.

"Take me home. We need to recover those cameras before sun-up," I said, trying to sit up. "Veronica, you have a concussion! You're going to have to stay put for at least one night, according to the attending nurse," he said sternly.

"Shit," I said, lying back in the bed. "You have to go get them," I whispered.

"But I'm not leaving you!"

"If you want to help me, go fetch the cameras now. Just be careful. Do you own a gun?"

"Do I look like the kind of person who owns a gun?" he asked sheepishly.

"You'd be surprised who owns a gun in this country. My Ruger is in the glove box of my RV. Go get it first before you get the cameras. And Mason? Be careful."

"Okay, I'll do it," he said.

He kissed me on the forehead and was gone.

I laid my head against the pillows. My head was throbbing, the room spinning in circles. I closed my eyes to stop the spinning, but then I saw the face of the man in the mask. I forced myself to keep them closed. As a therapist, I knew that facing trauma was the only way to overcome it. *But this isn't a patient, Veronica,* I reminded myself. *This is you!*

I squeezed my eyes shut tightly and the next thing I knew, I was asleep. Again.

# CHAPTER FORTY-NINE

When I woke up, the sun was shining, and a voluptuous, dark-skinned nurse was taking my vitals. I was immediately hit with a sense of duress. *Where was Mason? Why had he not returned?*

"I need my cell phone," I croaked at the nurse. She gave me a disapproving look, but then she retrieved a small plastic bag from the other side of the wooden table beside my hospital bed. "Thanks," I said, waiting for her to take the hint that I needed some privacy.

When she finally left, I retrieved my jeans from the bag and I located my cell phone in the left pants pocket. The screen was cracked from my tumble from the window, but it still seemed to be working.

I rapidly located Mason's name in the directory, and waited nervously for the phone to ring. It rang and rang, but he never picked up. I left a frantic message for him to call me.

I tried nearly half a dozen more times to reach

183

him. Something was wrong. I had sent Mason into the lion's den, and if something had happened to him, I would never forgive myself. I looked around at the machine and wires surrounding me. Only one of the wires was attached to me. The IV was in my forearm.

I squeezed my eyes shut, and pulled the needle out as quickly as possible. "Ouch!" I shouted, letting out a howl of pain. I sat there waiting, clutching my throbbing hand, anticipating that a nurse would hear my shout and come running, but no one came.

My head was woozy as I tried to stand up from the bed, and I gripped one of the metal sidebars carefully. I used my bloody hand to hold myself up and the other to pull on the filthy jeans and sweatshirt from last night. I did not see any socks in the bag, so I just slipped my Nikes on over my bare feet. My entire body felt like it had been hit by a Mack truck, and my hand was bleeding profusely. I grabbed a small hand towel from a stack on the shelf, and wrapped it around my hand.

I stuffed my cell phone into my pocket and I cracked open my hospital room door. The hallway was crammed with doctors and orderlies, but maybe that wasn't a bad thing. I could try to blend in. *With filthy clothes, a banged up face, and a bloody hand?* I scoffed at myself wearily. I had no choice but to go for it, though.

I straightened my gait and took a deep breath before plunging through the doorway. I walked down the hall like one of those speed walkers in the mall. I was a woman on a mission.

184

"Dr. von Derbach?" I heard a male voice call out from behind me. It was one of the doctors or nurses, no doubt. I took off in a sprint, charging through the heavy metal exit doors. I had no car and this didn't strike me as the kind of town that had cabs.

Down the street, I could see a grocery store and a couple of gas stations. I certainly didn't want to stand here in front of the hospital, so I jogged to the closest convenient store.

My head was pounding by the time I got there. I stopped and bent over, resting my hands on my knees. The bleeding had stopped, so I ditched the bloody towel in one of the garbage cans by the gas pumps. I took several deep, soothing breaths and looked around.

There were three cars in the gas station parking lot. A young gentleman wearing boots and a cowboy hat was climbing into a monstrous-sized truck. This was my opportunity.

"Hey!" I said, jogging up to him.

"I don't give money to hobos," he informed me sternly.

"I'm not homeless. I was just released from the hospital and I'm not from around here. Would you mind dropping me off at Lake Merlott? I'm staying with a friend in one of the lake houses…"

He eyed me suspiciously, but said, "Okey dokey," and I ran around to the passenger side. He had to get out and give me a boost because the truck was too high up for my meager height. It was quite embarrassing, but I had no time for vanity now. I had to get to Mason.

# CHAPTER FIFTY

The driver of the monster truck was Chris. As he pulled up in front of Mason's small lake house, I thanked him and lowered myself down to the ground as slowly, and least painfully, as possible. It still hurt like hell. Jumping to the pavement reminded me of the jump I was faced with last night, and I shuddered involuntarily.

As soon as Chris was gone, I started banging on Mason's door. After nearly ten minutes I realized that he was either not home or in some sort of trouble. I began circling the property, standing on my tip-toes to spy in his windows. I finally reached the window to his living room, and as I peered through the glass, I saw him sitting at his computer desk with the laptop open in front of him. His face was resting on the top of the desk, with his cheek pressed to its shiny veneer.

I held my breath. *Is he dead?*

But then I saw the small rhythmic rise and fall of his back, and I knew that he was breathing. I pounded on the window until he jumped with a start in the chair. He looked at me with my bruised face and wild hair, and I honestly don't think he recognized me for several seconds. Finally, he pointed a finger toward the front door, and I ran back around the house to meet him.

"Thank God, you're okay!" I exclaimed, throwing my arms around him.

"I must have fallen asleep while watching the footage from the cameras. I must have been more tired than I realized…" he admitted groggily.

After being up most of the night with me at the hospital, it wasn't all that surprising. "It's okay! I'm just so glad you have footage to review! Does that mean the attacker didn't destroy the cameras?" I asked hopefully.

"He took three cameras. I couldn't find a trace of them. I think he found those particular cameras because they were near the spot where you told me he attacked you. All of the others were still intact," he said quietly.

As I pictured my attacker taking those cameras, I thought about that thin, metal bat swinging down over my head, and the evil look in the eyes behind the mask. I shuddered once again.

"How much of it have you seen?" I asked, shaking off the memories.

"I know I watched for at least an hour before I passed out, but let's just review it all together again," he suggested, booting the laptop back up.

"You're amazing," I told him, reaching for him suddenly. I kissed him tenderly on the lips.

"I thought you might die. I was so scared," he admitted, kissing me back.

I couldn't stop kissing him, and the next thing I knew, we were tearing each other's clothes off. This wasn't the time for such an encounter, but the spontaneity of it was such a turn on.

As he pushed me toward the bed, I yelped in pain. My shoulders, back, and head still ached terribly from my fall.

"I'll be gentle," he whispered, and then he lifted me off my feet, carrying me straight to his bed.

# CHAPTER FIFTY-ONE

Mason was not simply the best lover I'd ever had; he was the *only* lover I'd had in nearly a decade. I yearned for more of him, and I didn't want the moment to end. But there was work to do. We had footage to examine and a homicidal maniac to watch out for. Most importantly, I had a son—dead or alive—to find.

We planted ourselves in front of the computer, and began the lengthy process of reviewing last night's activities on the video cameras. Nearly two hours in, which was around the time of my attack, we caught a glimpse of something on the camera. I wanted to see the image of my son. Instead, I saw the man who would haunt my nightmares for the rest of my life.

It was the man in the mask.

The image was dark and grainy, but it was a clear cut shot of him walking past the cameras, headed toward something or someone. *He's headed toward me*, I realized.

"This footage was taken right before he attacked me," I said frankly.

Mason stared at the screen in horror. "That bastard," he said, gritting his teeth together. I rested a hand on his shoulder.

"Freeze the image and zoom in as far as you can. Let's see if we can identify anything about him." Mason let out a worrisome sigh, but did as I requested.

As the image became larger and clearer, I felt a rising sense of terror in my chest. I was lucky to be alive, simple as that.

"It's definitely a man. Look at the size of those feet and his overall stature. Definitely a man," he repeated. I nodded in agreement.

My attacker's left hand was obscured from the camera. I couldn't see the bat since his hand was blocked. "Can you focus in more on the clothing and shoes?" I asked.

"I have it zoomed in as far as it will go. But let's print it off and examine it with a magnifying glass," he suggested smartly.

The printer roared to life, startling me. Mason held me tightly as we waited for the image to come through. *Would I ever recover from this?* I wondered. A voice inside my head reminded me that if I could recover from the death of my son, then I could recover from *anything. But have I really recovered from losing Sully? The answer was no*, I realized. *Quite possibly, I never would.*

The picture was done. Mason flipped on a small desk lamp and scrutinized it carefully with a magnifying glass. "Black shirt. Black pants. Black shoes," he said miserably. "Wait. It looks like there is some tiny stitching on the shirt. Is that an R?" I asked, squinting down at the photo.

We took turns looking at it from under the glass.

"Damn it!" I screamed angrily. "It's too far away to tell. We're getting nowhere!"

"Let's finish reviewing all of the tapes. Maybe, if we're lucky, we can catch another glimpse of him and see him from a better angle," Mason suggested. I nodded.

An hour and a half later, we were done with the videos and we still had nothing. I let out a frustrated groan.

"Now what?" I asked, running my fingers through my hair. I scratched at a patch of dry blood on my scalp.

"I have to go into work to repair something on the assembly line. It will take less than an hour. On my way there, I'll stop at the police department and drop off the photo to Sheriff Baggins. Maybe they can have an examiner blow the picture up better than I can," Mason said softly.

"I wouldn't count on that," I said miserably.

"Anyway, you're coming with me. I will not leave you alone," he said firmly.

I shook my head. "I'll wait here for you, Mason. I need to take a shower, and I want to write some notes down about what happened last night. If I think hard enough, maybe I can recall an important detail. Something I've possibly missed…"

The way he was looking at me, I could tell he didn't want to budge from his decision.

"The gun is here, remember? I promise I'll stay put and be on guard the entire time."

He finally relented. He tossed on a t-shirt and jeans, then kissed me goodbye.

I felt bad for lying to Mason, but I had to go get clean clothes from my camper and I wanted to do more investigating. I checked to make sure the Ruger was loaded and I slipped it into the back of my jeans before heading out to the woods.

# CHAPTER FIFTY-TWO

With the sun streaming through the pillow-like trees, and the sounds of boats on the water, this place didn't seem so frightening during the daytime. I made my way on foot over to where my RV was parked at the campsite. It was a weekday, which meant fewer campers, but the lake was dotted with fishermen and families enjoying the water.

I hurried out of the daylight and into the dark safety of my camper. I immediately froze, the hairs on my arms standing on end. Someone had been inside the camper.

Nothing appeared to be stolen, but my clothes and personal items were scattered throughout the RV. Someone wanted me gone from Lake Merlott; that much was certain.

The space in the camper was small, and there was basically nowhere for a person to hide, so I assumed my intruder was gone.

But my eyes slowly drifted to the one closet that

was big enough to hide a person—if they crouched and squeezed themselves inside it.

I removed the safety on the gun and gripped it in my hand.

When I was young, I hated guns. I even wrote a term paper once that ended with me ranting about how all of the weapons in the world should be thrown into a pile and destroyed. But something within me had changed long ago. I wish I could say it was simply the loss of my son, but that's not it. Working in the social work field should increase one's empathy, but it usually has the opposite effect. It had dulled me to other people's trauma, and with it, I had a reality check. There's no such thing as a perfect world, and idealism is just that: a concept.

I needed my gun for protection, and today I was grateful for it.

I threw open the closet door and aimed the gun straight at its contents. It was empty. I let out a deep whoosh of breath and sat down on my bed. For the first time in a long time, I let all of my grief, frustration, fear, and anger consume me. I wept into my hands uncontrollably.

My son was dead and someone was trying to kill me. Maybe it was the same person who killed my son. I wiped the tears and snot from my face, stiffening in anger as I thought of the man in the mask. If my attacker thought he could run me out of town by tossing around some crap in my camper, he was dead wrong.

# CHAPTER FIFTY-THREE

I showered quickly. If I had it my way, I'd stand under the blistering hot water for hours, but the old camper didn't hold much water and I needed to get a move on. When I stepped out of the shower, I twisted my wet hair into a no-nonsense bun and speedily brushed my teeth. My face, head, shoulders, legs, and back ached. *Everything* ached.

I slid on a pair of stretchy gym shorts and a short-sleeved tank. My Nikes were caked in mud, so I slid on an old back-up pair of Reeboks. I found my gun holster in one of my bedroom cabinets and I attached it to my hip, adding an extra magazine. I also placed a sharp pocket knife into my pocket.

I could remember one of my old patients telling me: "You should never bring a knife to a gun fight." *But it never hurts to have both*, I thought with a smile.

I grabbed my photo of Sully from the dash and stared at it for a few breathless moments. It was a

195

picture of him and Roxy on the tube. It was a blurry picture and it had been taken from a distance, but it was still my favorite picture because it was my last of Sully. I tucked the picture into my pocket.

I headed out to the woods, and made my way to the exact location where I was attacked. If Sheriff Baggins wasn't doing his job, I was going to do it for him.

I searched the ground for clues, hoping to find the metal bat or a DNA soaked cigarette butt, but I couldn't get that lucky.

Suddenly, there was a rustling of leaves behind me. I jerked around abruptly, whipping out the gun.

"Whoa! It's me!" Aubrey announced, putting up her hands like I was actually going to shoot her.

I lowered the gun.

"Sorry," I said, and I went back to searching.

"I heard what happened. You okay?" she inquired.

"Who told you?" I asked suspiciously.

"This is a small town. I overhead two cashiers talking about a doctor who was attacked in the woods by some rowdy teenagers. You're the only doctor I know of that's in these parts right now," she said, smiling grimly.

"It wasn't teenagers. It was a masked man. It was someone with something to hide," I said, placing my hands on my hips. She raised her eyebrows.

"What are you doing out here, Aubrey?" I asked wearily. I didn't mean to sound insensitive, but I didn't have much time before Mason got back, and I planned to hurry back to his house so I could pretend I'd never left it.

"Getting my pictures back from Cici," she said dully, holding up a stack of photographs.

"Was she able to identify your daughter as one of the ghosts she saw?" I asked, suddenly feeling like a bitch for being so brash with this poor woman.

"She's not sure. Cici is so old, and I could tell that all of my questions were wearing her out. I left the photos there for her to examine last night. When I picked them up just now, she said that she still wasn't sure if she'd seen her, and that she didn't want me getting my hopes up."

"May I take your pictures with me?" I asked, trying to sound gentle. "I'm going to search the woods all night and continue video-taping, regardless of what the prick who attacked me thinks. If I see her ghost, I'll know who she is from the photographs," I explained.

Aubrey's eyes brightened. "Maybe you're more of a believer than I thought…if you see her, please tell her not to run from me. I'm not afraid of ghosts, and I want a chance to communicate with her," she said, her face uncharacteristically animated as she talked about her daughter.

She handed me the stack of photos willingly. I stuck them into my knapsack carefully, pursing my lips as my heart ached for her. Like me, she had lost her greatest love in life.

"Do you want to help?" I asked. She nodded, eager to do something.

Aubrey and I spent the next thirty minutes searching the forest floor for clues. Finally, I told her that I had to get back to Mason's house. I promised to call her later. Hurrying back to his house, I was suddenly aware of the time. It had been slightly more than an hour since he left, and I had to hurry if I wanted to beat him there. I let out a sigh of relief as I realized his driveway was empty. He was still gone.

I let myself in and searched the house for any intruders with my gun in hand. It was all clear. I made sure all of the doors and windows were locked behind me, and then I lay down on his bed. It was the same spot where we'd made love, and I breathed in the smell of his salty sweetness.

My head started spinning again. I was still suffering from a concussion, I was sure of it.

I lay on the bed and closed my eyes, deciding to nap until he returned.

# CHAPTER FIFTY-FOUR

I woke up screaming with images of that dreadful closet, only this time there was no outlet at the top. I sat up, breathing heavily, but relieved by the familiar sight of Mason's bedroom.

But something was odd. I'd fallen asleep in the late afternoon, but now the room was cloaked in darkness. My eyes traveled through the open space, where it flowed into his dining space and living room. The whole house was dark, only electronics and moonlight casting shadows throughout the space.

I glanced at a bedside, digital alarm clock. It was nearly ten thirty. *How long had I been sleeping?* At least six hours, I realized. I felt around in the darkness for my gun. The feel of its velvety smoothness brought me some relief.

I wasn't too familiar with the landscape of Mason's house, and I had to run my hands along its walls, searching for a light switch. I finally hit pay dirt and I was rewarded by light. I walked through the house, flipping on all of the switches. Somehow, the brightness brought me great relief.

No matter how old we get, there's always an instinctual fear of the dark, I think.

Was it possible that Mason hadn't yet returned from work? Surely, he would have called by now, considering how concerned he had been for me earlier. I picked up my cell phone from the bed, and was just preparing to call him, when I noticed a fast food bag on the kitchen counter. I walked over to inspect it; I didn't recall it being there earlier. I peeked inside the sack. It was filled with cold hamburgers and hardened fries.

Next to the food bag was a handwritten note. I'd never seen Mason's handwriting before, and I was shocked by how messy it was. The words were written in bright red ink. It said:

*I saw you were sleeping and didn't want to wake you up. Going to the drugstore to buy you some Tylenol.*

*–Mason*

I breathed a sigh of relief. It was kind of him to let me sleep but he knew I wanted to investigate again tonight. I tried not to be irritated, but I had to admit I was slightly perturbed. I opened his refrigerator and pulled out an icy can of soda. I popped the top and chugged it while I leaned against the counter in front of the sink.

I hadn't realized how dehydrated I was. I was

just about to warm up one of the cold burgers, when I saw Mason's backpack on the floor by the note. I'd only known the man for a couple short days, but he always carried that backpack with him. *Was he in such a big hurry to go to the drugstore that he accidentally left the bag behind?*

I found the trash can and threw my can away. I strolled around the empty house, looking at his paintings and photographs. He truly was a magnificent artist. I headed back to the kitchen and I stared at the words on the note. Something felt strange.

Impulsively, I lifted the heavy backpack off the floor. I carried it to the kitchen table and unzipped it. I paused before pulling the two sides apart.

I'd never been the type of person who took it upon themselves to snoop. I'd never even done it to Sully. *Perhaps you should have paid more attention with Sully*, I scolded myself.

I peered down into the bag. I was astonished to see a bag filled with broken cameras. Mason had specifically told me that the cameras had been taken, and he'd found no trace of them. When had he found these?

I pulled them out and peered back into the bag. I leapt back, releasing a blood curdling scream. Lying in the bottom of the backpack was the black leather mask, the same one that haunted my dreams.

# CHAPTER FIFTY-FIVE

I dropped the bag, grabbed my own knapsack, and ran like hell out of there. I held onto the gun as I raced to Mason's closest neighbor. The two houses nearest to him were the ones that were vacant. I cringed as I passed the house where I was held captive last night.

The sight of Marlene's bungalow up ahead provided some solace. I couldn't wrap my brain around this. *Why would Mason try to kill me? Could he really be some sort of psychopath?*

I started banging on Marlene's door, keeping watch for Mason's red Jeep. I had to call the police immediately. Marlene looked at me with a stunned expression, probably because of last night's bruises on my face and my bewildered demeanor.

"Please let me in," I pleaded. She opened her door and I darted inside. I locked her door behind me. "Are there any other entrances? If so, please make sure they're locked."

"What in God's name is going on, Veronica?" she asked, her eyes widened in fear.

"Please just lock the back door first," I pleaded. I followed her to the back door and observed as she bolted the lock in place.

"Now tell me what's going on," she said nervously. I told her about last night's attack, and about the mask and cameras at Mason's house.

"Oh, dear!" she exclaimed, pacing back and forth across the threadbare carpet of her living room.

"We must call the police. Now," I told her. She nodded. She walked over to a home phone attached to her kitchen wall, and called the sheriff's department.

I listened as Marlene relayed my story to one of Sheriff Baggins' deputies. "They'll be here in ten minutes," she informed me.

"Thank you," I said, embracing the woman awkwardly. "May I use your restroom?" I asked, eager to relieve my bladder and dig through my knapsack for my cell phone. She pointed to a door in the hall.

I sat on the toilet, taking deep breaths. My head was still swimming with doubts about Mason's guilt, but I urged myself to let the police handle it. I couldn't take any chances after what happened to me last night.

Anxiously, I started digging through my deep knapsack, trying to find the small flip phone. I had to call Dr. Paddison. I still wasn't sure what was going on here, but I was sure that I needed her help. The phone wasn't in my bag, and I suddenly remembered that I'd left it on Mason's bed.

*At least I remembered the gun.*

As I went to close the knapsack, Aubrey's stack of pictures caught my eye. One of the pictures in particular...it was one of her daughter, Isabel, riding on a tube attached to the back of a boat. Aubrey had obviously snapped the picture from the backend of a boat, and the angle of it reminded me of the one I'd taken of Sully the day he died.

I unfolded Sully's picture from my back pocket, and I held both photos side by side. It wasn't just the fact that they were both tubing in their photos; the backgrounds of each picture looked identical. *Why do they look so similar to me?* I wondered, staring intensely at them both.

Then I saw it. A pink and white pontoon boat far in the distance, captured in *both*—my picture of Sully and Aubrey's picture of Isabel. I shook my head, confused.

I mean, it was possible that whoever owned the pink and white boat spent a lot of time at Lake Merlott, and had just happened to be in the background in both photographs.

*What a bizarre coincidence!* I pondered. But I didn't believe in coincidence...

I stared at both photos until they turned fuzzy.

I'd seen that boat before, parked by one of the resident's boat docks.

My head was so confused from yesterday's concussion, and I struggled to get my thoughts straight. I knew where I'd seen the boat before. I turned the sink faucet on for noise and I crept over to the bathroom window. The window looked out toward the back of the house, and even from here, I could see the boat parked in the back. It was anchored right next to the dock.

*What the hell is going on? Mason and now Marlene? Was I losing my freaking mind?*

I remembered that Marlene had a husband. *What was his name?* I searched the inner workings of my brain, struggling to recall it. It started with an R. Rick! Oh, God. The stitching on the masked man's shirt in the picture…

I remembered the day that I came to Marlene's house. She said that her husband Rick was in the basement whittling wood. *Wood*…

I was suddenly overwhelmed by images of the masked man leaning over me, preparing to strike me with the bat. He had a distinct smell. Right before I went unconscious, I'd been hit with the strong smell of wood shavings.

# CHAPTER FIFTY-SIX

I knew I couldn't face Marlene without giving my feelings away. *I wonder if she knows what her husband did to me.* But then I instantly waved that thought aside. Of course she knew. Wives always know their husbands' misdoings.

If I couldn't leave the bathroom, there was only one way out of here. The last thing I wanted to do was climb through another damn window, but I didn't see any other way. At least this window was located on the ground floor.

I slid the window up slowly, trying not to make a sound. The water in the sink was still running. I lifted myself up, and started pulling myself through the window. Just as I was about to make it through, I heard Marlene behind me. She must have had a key to the bathroom door, I realized. She was going to kill me before the police arrived.

Who was I kidding? There was no way that woman called the cops. It must have all been for show. I started wriggling through the window frantically, but I felt her grab my leg. She started to pull me back through the window, but I held steadfastly to its sill. I started kicking my free leg with all of my might until I felt it connect with something. Marlene let out a small, painful cry. She released my other leg, and I fell out the window face first.

I pulled myself up and started running. I could hear her screaming Rick's name in the distance. I knew the man in the mask was coming for me, and it certainly wasn't Mason. How could I have been so wrong?

# CHAPTER FIFTY-SEVEN

It was only a matter of seconds before I heard heavy footsteps behind me. He was coming. "Come back here, bitch!" he yelled behind me. He was not right behind me, but he wasn't all that far away, either.

I ran like a madwoman, stumbling in the dark over fallen tree branches and shrubbery. I would have loved to have a flashlight right now, but it would probably have given away my location.

I kept running, trying to make it to the Tanners' house or Aubrey's small mansion. But just as I was getting close, I heard and sensed him right behind me. "There you are," a deep, gravelly voice said from behind me. I didn't have any time to think. I ran straight for the lake and dove in. He couldn't find me if I was underwater, at least that's what I was hoping for.

# CHAPTER FIFTY-EIGHT

I swam until I thought my lungs would burst, and then I forced myself to swim some more. I refused to break the surface until I had distanced myself significantly from the shore and until my lungs forced me to breathe.

I swam with my eyes open, but the water was murky and colorless. I tentatively lifted my head in the darkness, and sucked in a deep breath of air. I had not heard anyone dive in behind me, but there was no way to be certain until it was too late. I looked for the other side of the lake. It seemed liked miles away in the distance.

I pressed on, forcing my body to pull forward breathlessly. When I felt on the verge of passing out, I lifted my head for air again. I saw the northwest shore directly up ahead, and I saw no signs of anyone or anything on the bank. I went for it.

When I thought it was safe, I dug myself out of

the muddy water and pulled myself onto the bank. I army crawled into the woods, and I sat up on my knees, crouching behind a bush. I pulled the wet gun from the holster. Would it work if it wasn't dry? I wasn't certain. I could only pray that it would if I needed it to.

That's when I heard a loud grunt, and I saw a man pulling himself onto the shore, just as I had moments earlier. He was tall and muscular, much younger than Marlene. He wasn't wearing a mask, but I could tell by his size and build that it was my captor from last night.

# CHAPTER FIFTY-NINE

The safety was off and I used my other hand to steady my gripping hand.

"Where are you at, you stupid bitch?" he yelled, scanning the trees with his beady, evil eyes. I stayed perfectly still. "Come out, come out, wherever you are!" he said, grinning maniacally. He was trying to provoke me, but I kept perfectly still, barely breathing.

He stood silently, only a few yards away from me. Like a predator, he sniffed at the air and scanned the trees again. His eyes passed right over where I was, crouched behind a short bush.

I held my breath, never moving my gun from where it was aimed at his head. "I know where you are..." he said, taunting me. "Your sweetheart, Mason, is tied up at the house. If you ever want to see him again, you better show yourself. Unless you want him to end up like your son!"

This is the part when I should have jumped up

crazily, begging for him to release Mason and asking him if he killed my son. But I wouldn't give this bastard the satisfaction. I stepped out from my hiding spot and pulled the trigger, aiming straight for the bastard's head.

# CHAPTER SIXTY

My goal was to blow his damn head off, this possible murderer of my son, kidnapper of Mason, and almost murderer of me, but unfortunately, my aim wasn't spot on. The bullet hit his neck area, but he didn't go down. He gripped the side of his neck, and charged straight for me like a mad bull.

I ran right past him, and dove back into the dark lake water. He may have still been alive, but I knew there was no way he could outswim me, or possibly swim at all, in his physical state. I knew where I was going this time. I'd seen a speed boat parked at a dock in the distance, and I swam straight for it, never looking back as I stroked the water desperately.

By the time I made it to the sleek, two-seater speedboat, my legs felt like Jell-O and my breath was raspy and strained. The dock had a ladder, thankfully, so I climbed up it and jumped into the boat. I'd been counting on the keys being in it, and on this occasion, I was in luck. I turned the key, and the engine roared to life.

I'd only driven my father's boat on a few occasions, but I handled it like a pro. I backed it up, spun the wheel, and soared across the surface of the black lake. Moments later, I'd reached Marlene and Rick's dock.

I know Marlene could see me coming, but I honestly did not care. I wouldn't hesitate to shoot her either at this point. I was headed back into the lion's den. I had to make sure that Mason was okay, and end this thing once and for all.

# CHAPTER SIXTY-ONE

Driving a boat is one thing; parking it is a whole different type of feat. I couldn't take my time here; doing so might just get me killed. I slammed it into the dock's side, and jumped off the side of the boat carelessly. Whoever's boat it was, I would reimburse them later. I used the ladder on Marlene and Rick's dock to pull myself up, and I slowly crept forward.

As I approached the house, I heard Marlene's voice call out to me, "Where's Rick, you crazy bitch? If you did anything to hurt him, I'll skin you alive!" she screamed.

"Where is Mason?" I asked quietly, searching for her location in the dark. The house was shrouded in darkness. I looked left and right, and back again. Why did she have all of the lights off?

"Tell me where Rick is!" she screamed, panic rising in her voice.

"I killed him," I said, still searching for her in the

215

dark. The next thing I knew, a gun shot rang out, and a bullet whizzed right by my ear. Then another one and another one. This crazy bitch was shooting at me!

I would have expected Rick to shoot at me, but this was a surprise. I wanted to shoot back at her, but I couldn't see her, and the last thing I needed to do was waste ammo. I hid behind a tree, pressing my back to it and holding my breath.

Where the hell were all of the neighbors? Surely, someone had to hear gunfire and they'd hopefully called the police. Another shot rang out, and this one was close. She was headed straight for me!

I took off running again, this time back toward Mason's and Cici Gray's houses. That's when I felt a bullet slam into my backside, and my body slumped to the ground.

# CHAPTER SIXTY-TWO

I was down but not out. I dug my fingers into the dry, flaky earth of the forest floor, and I drug my body forward. I used my elbows to crawl, and I tried to pull my body along, but I could barely feel the lower half of my body. *I've been shot,* I realized, still in shock from the impact.

My vision was narrowed and spotty. *Please, don't pass out again, Veronica!* I begged myself.

"Follow me," said a voice. I looked up to see a teenage boy. It wasn't my son.

The boy's face was peering out of a manmade hole in the forest floor. "Who are you?" I asked, inching my way closer to him. More bullets rang through the air, and I slipped down into the hole just before I got shot again.

# CHAPTER SIXTY-THREE

The next thing I knew, I was being drug by my arms through a narrow, dirt tunnel in the ground. Was this really happening? Perhaps I was dead and this was the route to hell.

The dirt-lined tunnel was so narrow that if it got any tighter, I would be stuck completely. I imagined myself being squeezed from all sides, squished like an encapsulated sardine. There was dirt in my hair and eyes, and my wound ached painfully. For what seemed like a mile, my body was inched along this tight space. The boy that pulled me, this savior of mine, only spoke once to say, "Be quiet. We can't afford for her to hear us."

Eventually the tiny space seemed to widen, and I was lifted down into a cavernous space. For such a small hole, the space that it opened into was shockingly enormous. Another boy, who looked similar to the first, laid me on my back on the floor. The two boys stood over my limp figure on the concrete floor.

"We can't hide her here, Rex! They'll be down here to check on us in an hour! We had it all planned out, and now it's all going to be for nothing!"

The boy who saved me, Rex I presume, said, "What was I supposed to do? Let her die?!"

Speaking of dying, I thought that I might. "I'm shot. You have to call for help," I said in barely a whisper. Both boys stared at me wordlessly for several seconds. "Call for help? Lady, I wish it were only that easy. I've been trapped down here for God knows how long. That's why we've been using our hands to dig the tunnels. We dug this one and another one on the other side of the lake. This tunnel was our only hope. But now the old lady is going to kill us for sure. Just like she did the others..."

It suddenly dawned on me who these boys were: Rex and Albert Shaw. "Do you know my son, Sully?" I asked, my eyes widening in fear and amazement. I suddenly felt a rush of energy flow through my weakened body. Both boys stared at me with an odd, tranquil expression, and my heart skipped a beat.

# CHAPTER SIXTY-FOUR

"Please, I must see my son," I cried, trying to pull myself up despite the searing pain in my back. The boys looked at each other, confused. "You're Sully's mother?" Albert asked, scratching his head.

I didn't have time for their questions. I was dying here and my son was alive! "Take me to my son!" I demanded, clenching my teeth in pain and frustration. "Mom, I'm here," a voice said from behind me.

I jerked around and came face to face with my son. "Sully!" I screamed. He was older and thinner, with a gaunt, sickly look to him, but he was perfect all the same. He hadn't grown as much as he should have in five years. He seemed so fragile and pale. He placed a finger to his lips, shushing me.

"But, how?" I cried, reaching out for him.

"Shhh. We don't have time for this. These boys have been digging this tunnel for years with their bare hands. If she sees you down here, it will all be in vain. She's killed before, and she'll kill again. You have to go back through the hole and get help."

"Come with me now," I pleaded, cupping his beautiful face in my hands. "One of us can't walk," he said grimly, motioning with his thumb toward a bed in the back. There was someone lying on top of the mattress, someone limp and lifeless. "We were waiting for her to heal before we left. Go now, Mom! Please!" he begged.

Albert and Rex were staring at my wound, panic-stricken. "I don't know if she'll make it, man," Albert said. "She's been shot." Sully's face contorted with pain. He rolled me onto my side and examined the wound on my back. "The bullet is lodged inside of you. If it wasn't for that, you already would have bled to death," he said grimly.

"I'm going now," I said firmly. I kissed my darling son on the cheek, and let them lift me back into the hole.

# CHAPTER SIXTY-FIVE

I edged my way through the hole, gasping for air. I dug at the dirt in this manmade hole, dragging my body back up. If it wasn't for the safety of my son, I don't know that I would have made it back through. The top of the hole had been left uncovered, and I prayed that Marlene had not yet discovered it. I cautiously poked my head through the hole, sucking in breaths of cool, fresh air. There was a large piece of driftwood lying next to the opening, and I assumed this was how they covered up its entrance.

I pulled myself up, and slid the piece of wood onto the top of the opening. I thought about those young children, including my son, digging this tunnel in the ground. The thought of it was unbearable. The fact that my son had been here, alive, at the lake this whole time, was traumatizing for me. The reality of this had still not sunk in, and probably never would.

I wouldn't lose my son again, not this time. I turned around, and was met face to face with a shotgun.

# CHAPTER SIXTY-SIX

Marlene stood at the end of the gun, and her husband was right beside her. He was still clutching the bloody wound on his neck. "Don't make a sound. Walk," Marlene said, jabbing me with the butt of the gun.

"Which way?" I asked wearily.

"Shut your mouth. To our house," Rick said, shoving me backwards again. The fact that they were waiting for me to come out of that hole made me realize that the jig was up. They knew what the children had done, and they were most certainly going to dispose of them at their first opportunity.

My gun was gone; it had fallen onto the ground when I was shot. I scanned the ground with my eyes, hoping to catch a glimpse of it as I trudged along with the shotgun pointed at my backside. As my eyes followed the ground, I realized that the dirt tunnel led not to an underground cavern below their house, but from the vacant house that I was trapped in last night. To think I'd been so close to my son the whole time was devastating.

They pushed me into their home through a back door. I gasped as I saw Mason, lying lifeless on the floor.

# CHAPTER SIXTY-SEVEN

"Don't worry, we didn't kill him yet. We were waiting for you before we did that. I want you to watch while I kill your nosy boyfriend. I caught him putting up more cameras, and I knew you two relentless assholes just wouldn't quit," Rick said, chuckling maniacally.

"I hit him over the head before he even saw it coming!" he boasted, roaring with laughter.

"Are you the one who left me the note and put the mask in his backpack? Why didn't you just kill me when you had the chance?" I asked. "Why all the fun and games?" I wasn't really interested in his answers; I only needed to stall for time.

"Because I couldn't go chopping you up in somebody's random house, and I knew you'd come running straight to me, like the good, little idiot that you are. Now, I have a plastic-filled room waiting for you downstairs, baby," he said, rubbing his hands on my chest grotesquely. "You sick freaks!" I

226

screamed angrily, shoving his hands away.

"So, I guess you saw the darling children?" Marlene asked, staring at me with eyes filled with hatred. "You're going to watch those kids die too," she said sinisterly. She was proving to be just as psychopathic as her darling husband.

"How did you take him from the water?" I asked, again stalling for time.

Marlene let out a loud, throaty chuckle. "I didn't take him. He came to me, just like you did," she said, smiling at me with a look of self-satisfaction.

What on earth was she talking about? This woman truly was insane!

"He swam to the shore and came to your house, and then you did what? Made him your freaking prisoner? You're insane!" I shouted, eager to strangle this bitch.

She clucked her tongue and wiggled one finger back and forth. "Nope. That's not it, either," she taunted cruelly.

"Then what, you lunatic? Why did you take my son?"

"He found us on the Internet. We set up a chat room for children who wanted to run away from home, and your son contacted *us*. The whole thing was a set up. He's the one who suggested his grandfather ask you to take the trip. He chose the fishing spot, and we stayed close behind in our boat. The storm was just a crazy coincidence, but it worked out superbly for the storyline. He poured a vial of his blood down the side of the boat, just like he'd been instructed, and when the current got rough, he jumped while the waters were just right.

We picked him up on our boat. The original plan was for him to fall off while tubing like the other kid did, but I think he chickened out at first. We helped orchestrate the plan, but he executed it. He didn't even want you. We promised to give him money and a car to start his own life, but that was just a ploy to get him here."

*To get all of them here*, I thought, thinking of the other children in that dark, dreadful cellar space.

She continued, "I thought Sully would want to stay when he got here, and I wanted him to be a good son. But he wasn't. Just like all the others. I've spared a small handful of them and kept them fed. They should be grateful that I haven't killed them yet. I learned my lesson and this time, they're all going to die. Your son deserved what he got..." Marlene said, smiling evilly.

"But you're going to die first," Rick said, taking me by the arms. He pushed me into a dark room, and Marlene followed behind. When the lights came on, it was filled with plastic, just as Rick had promised.

Rick and I stood there, facing each other. "First, let's have a little fun," he said, walking toward me slowly. He commanded me to remove my clothing.

"May I turn around?" I asked shyly.

He laughed. "Being modest at a time like this is stupid, but sure, go right ahead." As I turned around, I felt him close behind me, breathing down my neck.

I reached into my pocket and gripped the knife in my hand. I jerked around unexpectedly and jabbed the knife straight into his jugular. Blood spurted out, hitting my face and spraying the plastic-coated walls. Marlene stood behind him, gaping at me in horror. I gave her no time to react. I charged at her like a wild bull, punching her in the gut.

I slammed the door to the room behind me, leaving her inside. I wasn't shocked to see a lock on the outside of the door in this house of horrors. I locked the door and pulled a heavy dresser in front of it, blocking her in.

The phone on the wall was a few feet away. I dialed 911 and calmly told them I had two murderers locked in a room. I gave them my exact location. As I waited for them to come, I ran to check on Mason. He was unconscious, but breathing.

I ran outside of the house and tried the house next door. The door was locked, so I picked up one of those fake welcome rocks, and used it to smash in the nearest window. I brushed glass aside, and climbed into an empty living room space.

I quickly found a pair of stairs that led to a basement. Marlene and Rick must obviously own this property too, I realized. They made sure no one discovered their evil secret by not even keeping the children in their own home. There was a heavy steel door at the bottom of the steps and it was secured by a rusty padlock.

I searched the house for some sort of tool that would help me break down the door. But then it dawned on me that there must be a key. I knew that Marlene must have it somewhere. I ran back to their house, and I grabbed every single key off of the key rack, and I carried them all back with me.

I raced back down the stairs, and I tried every single one until I found the key that took me to my son. The room below was a chamber of horrors. I'd been in it earlier, but I hadn't realized how horrendous it truly was. The walls were made of concrete, and dingy mattresses were strewn across the floor. They were using a small bucket as a toilet. The space stank of excrement and death.

The Shaw boys and Sully were waiting for me. "Come on! The police on their way," I told them, smiling at my son gaily. "We can't leave Isabel," one of the Shaw boys whined. He led me to a dark corner where she lay on a dirty old mattress. Aubrey's daughter was alive, but she certainly didn't look well. Her skin was gray and covered in bed sores. I wondered how much longer she had before death consumed her.

Suddenly, I heard police sirens in the distance. I didn't want to leave my son's side, but I had to go meet the police. "You can stay with her. I'll send the EMS workers down here to get her," I assured him. I raced back up the stairs to meet the police. But first, I turned back to look at my son. "I'm so sorry, Sully. Everything is going to be okay from here on out, I promise. I will make up for all of my mistakes, and I will never let anyone hurt you again."

# CHAPTER SIXTY-EIGHT

By the time the police got to Rick, he was dead and gone. I don't think anyone will be shedding any tears over that one. Except Marlene. She spends all of her days now in her own chamber of doom, and she will soon be put to death.

Mason spent most of that first week in the hospital. The doctors thought he may never wake up, but he did—just as I came out of surgery for my gunshot wound.

Aubrey's daughter stayed in the hospital substantially longer than the rest of us. As the only female in that hole, she endured the worst of it. She was sick with a terrible bout of pneumonia and had a broken leg that had never healed properly. Apparently, at some point, Marlene had thrown her down a set of stairs. Isabel was eventually released into the loving arms of her mother, Aubrey. The happy, smiling woman who reunited with her daughter bore little resemblance to the dejected,

231

sullen woman I'd met that day at the lake. She had her baby back, and that was all that mattered to her.

Rex and Albert's father's reaction to being reunited with his sons was the greatest shock for me. The same man who called his sons 'no-good sons of bitches' when I asked him about their death, fell to the ground and bawled like a baby as he held his sons in his arms. I suppose I shouldn't have judged his reaction that day. We all deal with grief differently. He chose to do it with anger.

Tommy Mitchell, Cynthia Thomas, and Mandy Munfer's parents were not so lucky. Their skeletal remains were unearthed from Marlene and Rick's backyard. I don't even want to know how they died, and honestly, I've never asked. I never will.

Their parents were finally able to bury the bodies, but it would never be enough. I mourned for the parents the most. I knew what it was to experience loss.

As it turned out, Rick and Marlene were actually named Michael and Sandy Rainey. They changed their names nearly fifteen years ago, when this whole thing at Lake Merlott began. Rick and Marlene were merely their online aliases.

Rick and Marlene's two children ran away from them nearly twenty years ago. After that, they apparently began their insane mission to replace their children with runaways. I wondered where their real children were now, and if they were watching the news. They were smart enough to get away from a set of parents, who I am certain, were already crazy before they ran away.

The therapist in me can't help but wonder about

all of the pathology behind Rick and Marlene's crazy kidnapping/killing scheme, but the mother in me doesn't give a damn. Who cares why they were so crazy? I'm just thankful that they are gone, and will no longer hurt innocent children, like my beautiful son. My son didn't deserve what happened to him, and no amount of thoughtful analysis will make it seem like anything other than a senseless crime to me.

So, I told you what happened with the other families. But this is what happened with mine…on the day of the rescue, I was loaded into an ambulance, and taken away from my son. When I woke up lying in that hospital bed, I was relieved to see him again. He sat by my bedside, stroking my fingers and arms, humming a soft lullaby that I had sung to him when he was young. The song was achingly beautiful, and for several minutes, I laid there, pretending to sleep as I listened.

"I'm so sorry for leaving you, Mom…" he said, staring down at my hands. I put up a hand to stop him, but he shushed me, and went on: "Teenagers can be so stupid sometimes, and I was the dumbest of them all. I was angry with you for so many little reasons, and I thought I'd found a way out, to be with my girlfriend and be all grown up on my own. I thought I was invincible. I wish I would have never done this…I wish I could take it all back…" he lamented.

"No, Sully. Every single bit of this is my fault. I shoulder all of the blame, and rightfully so. I should have been a better mother. I never should have let you get away. I never should have stopped

233

searching, or given up hope. Now that I have you back, I'm going to give up ghost hunting and buy us a nice, new house," I promised, tears flowing down my cheeks, burning my cracked, dry lips.

"But you can't give up ghost hunting, Mom. You are so damned good at it," he said, leaning forward in his chair with a grave expression.

"But I'm not, Sully," I said, laughing tearfully. "In fact, I've never seen a ghost in all of these years."

"But you found me, Mom," he said pointedly.

"Yes, I found you. I solved the mystery. But this whole 'searching for ghosts' nonsense, I'm done with it. I'm going to focus on you, and I'll spend the rest of my life making up my mistakes to you."

"You already have, Mom. I love you," Sully said, kissing me tenderly on the cheek. He held his lips on my forehead, lingering on the moment.

I closed my eyes, sucking in the sweet smells of my son, flashes of memories darting through my mind. Blue cake batter, falling stars, swing sets, bike rides, bruised knees, beautiful laughter...all of my memories of him, *our* memories, dancing through my thoughts. "I will never forget one moment that I've spent with you, Sully. You were my first true love, and you will be my last."

But then I opened my eyes and the moment was gone. My son was gone with it.

# EPILOGUE

A month after Mason and I purchased our first home together, I received a call from Dr. Paddison. We'd just settled down to dinner, and I immediately regretted taking the call.

"I know you're taking some time off, understandably, but there are still several clients requesting your services. Mayor Fish spread the news of what you do for a living, and requests for help have increased astronomically. Some of these cases sound serious, Veronica. One of the clients even claims that a poltergeist almost killed his youngest child."

I listened to her, biting my lip thoughtfully. It was only two months ago that my son's body was unearthed from the ground, his bones and clothing found only a short, half mile away from the others. He had been dead for at least two years.

I was happy for the Shaws and Aubrey for finding their children alive, and I could only wish that I'd been so lucky. Those three surviving children all reported seeing the ghost of my son in the dark, horrific chamber. According to them, my son is the one who helped them dig the tunnels. He told the other children that I was coming to save them. *A born leader*—that was the Sully I loved.

The way he described me to them, he made me sound like a super hero. I've never felt so proud of him. He kept those children alive by giving them hope and guiding them out of the darkness.

Getting to see my son, even if he was a ghost, had changed my whole life for the better. I now knew the answer to what had happened to my son, and in searching for his ghost, he had led me to the other children, the ones who still had a chance. I know that my son's life was cut short, and I'll never understand it fully, but I know that he is out there somewhere, serving some greater purpose than he did here on Earth. I was lucky to have him in my life for as long as I did.

Last week, Mason suggested that we try to have a child. It's something that I have never considered. I'm not ready yet, but I'm seriously thinking about it. I somehow know that Sully would approve.

"You should go to Dr. Paddison. Get your next cases. Hell, I'll even go with you if you want. I'll just bring my artwork with me," Mason said softly from behind me as I hung up with Dr. Paddison. He wrapped his arms around me, squeezing me tenderly. Nowadays, I don't know what I would do without this man.

"Yes, Mom. Go…" said another voice in my ear, but Sully was nowhere to be found. I smiled up toward the sky, wishing my son was truly here in the flesh with me. I could have sworn that I heard another voice say, "I am here. I always will be, Mom…"

That night I packed my suitcase, and the next morning, Mason and I loaded up the RV. I'd gotten so used to running—but why was I running this time? *Run toward a better life, not away from the old one,* I could hear Sully saying.

As we pulled out of the driveway, I glanced in the rearview mirror. For a brief second, I saw my son.

***The End***

Check out a sneak peek of Carissa's newest novel,
a paranormal romance story.

***Sneak Peek***

# Midnight Moss

*I can still remember what it feels like.*

*The sting of the blow...before it even really hit me.*

*Like energy in the air between us, leaving his fist and bursting through my cheek before it even connected.*

*That energy, that hate—that is what caused the greatest sting. That is what left its mark...even when evidence of the mark was gone, still the burning remained.*

*My cheek sore, the skin felt tight around the bruise, but lumpy.*

*But now there is soft wet grass against the backs of my thighs, cool black earth that squishes beneath my toes, soft at the edge of my spine. Digging my heels in and letting my back sink further...I become one with the ground.*

*The cool wet blades envelop me like a soft, sweet blanket, and for a moment, ever so brief, all of the pain is forgotten.*

*Every last wound has healed.*

My dreams were muddled and strange, and I woke up confused about where I was, my skin damp to the touch, just like it was in my dream. Tiny beads of sweat clung to my lower lip as I struggled

1

to pull the sticky blankets away from my skin.

Glancing around my grandma's bedroom—my bedroom—I saw that it was light outside. Not just light, but very light, like maybe it was well past noon.

My phone showed no missed calls from my mother. That surprised me. I had expected her to worry about me not calling...

The signal still failing, I made my way downstairs, trying to find a spot—any spot—where I could get a bar of service.

Finally, I gave up, making my way toward the kitchen. Vowing to switch cell phone carriers first thing, I opened up a box of Honey Combs and dumped them in a bowl, just as I remembered that I had no milk to eat them with.

Frustrated, I set the bowl aside. Without my car or a working phone, I felt a little helpless here.

I got dressed for the day. I chose a pair of thin tights and a ripped Fiona Apple tank, then tied up my running shoes.

It's only a few miles to get to town. It won't take me that long, I tried to assure myself. Although fall was fast approaching, the air felt as warm and sticky as maple syrup. I was grateful to have chosen the tank top.

After locking up, I ran swiftly down the hill, my Nikes crunching against tiny leaves and loose gravel. Eyeing the creepy gravestones, I turned right, passing a large rose bed and eventually a few dilapidated mailboxes. The old farmhouses they belonged to looked identical to one another, with deep lots, peeling paint, and overgrown lawns.

I knew there was a town close by because I'd passed it when Nolan and I drove through yesterday.

Not one car passed by on the road, and for a minute I felt a sense of vertigo as I pounded the monotonous pavement. There were no signs, so I couldn't even tell what road I was on.

The bright afternoon sun was at its hottest, and I could feel the burn, not only from the heat, but also because I hadn't run like this since high school. My thighs and knees were killing me.

Too slow to be a track star in high school, I liked to venture out after the team was done practicing, using the laps to clear my head and keep my body in shape. But it had been at least six months since I'd gone on a run like this.

Running was a way to void out my thoughts and let my feet do all the work. I used to imagine all of my worries dripping down from my head to my feet, while my feet beat the crap out of them.

Vegetation grew thinner as I neared town. But instead of following the road, I suddenly surprised myself by veering to the left and racing through a gap between two poplar trees. I ducked beneath branches, leaped over a small babbling creek, and darted up, and then down, a weathered rocky hill, stopping as I came face to face with a chain-linked fence.

Gasping for breath, I leaned against the twisted wires, peering through to the other side.

It was almost like I knew where I was going. Like my feet were guiding me without any control of my own...

But that's silly, I realized, feeling foolish. I've never gone down that road before, and I've never seen this fence either...

The fence was twice as tall as me, with what appeared to be barbed wire lining the top. To prevent people from climbing over, I supposed.

As far as I could tell, the fence stretched for miles, both east and west. There has to be an end to it somewhere. But if there is, I can't see it from here...

There was nothing much to see on the other side of the fence, just wild plants and massive trees, almost like a wild jungle. The thick vines and trees were fighting to break through the metal grates that contained them.

If someone had property on the other side, they sure as hell weren't taking care of it.

I walked east along the fence line, running my fingers across the metal links, and sidestepping thick black roots and rocks. I tried to see through the wild forest, catch a glimpse of what lie beyond the foliage.

Then suddenly, a flash of light sparkled through the trees, reflecting off a body of water. A lake or pond, I realized. I couldn't see more than a sliver of it, but there was definitely water beyond the fence.

The sound of a dog barking caused me to jump back. Feeling ridiculous, I looked around for the animal, not seeing one. I couldn't tell if the steely bark had come from my side of the fence, or the other.

"Oh, well." I headed back out the way I came, and I got back on the road. My momentum gone, I walked slowly the rest of the way to town, wishing I'd thought to bring a bottle of water.

Finally, I was relieved to see a single row of shops, a gas station, a church, and a food mart. Around the corner were two tiny brick buildings— they looked like schools, based on their utilitarian design.

I made my way toward the nearest store front. Beyond the small stretch of buildings, there were six or seven streets of tiny houses—Black Cat Springs's "suburbs," I presumed.

K-Mart. It was the tiniest one I'd ever seen, with only a small scattering of cars in the lot, but I was happy to see it. I made a beeline for it.

The icy blast from the air conditioning felt so good, I nearly moaned with pleasure as I crossed through the double glass doors. I grabbed a small shopping basket, smiling at a Hispanic gentleman who was working the door. Halloween decorations dotted the aisles—plastic pumpkins, scarecrows, and cackling skeletons.

My plan was to head straight toward the food section, in hopes of finding milk and bread, but as soon as I saw the home improvement section, I veered off impulsively.

Kmart's paint selection was dismal, but I immediately honed in on a bright turquoise color. It would look great in the living room, but first I'd have to remove all that wall paper...

Picking up the can of paint, I saw it was labeled 'Peacock Blue.'

"Go figure," I said, smirking, as I remembered my grandma's peacock box.

5

"May I help you?"

The voice was deep, gravelly. I turned around to see an employee—a guy with dark brown hair and a stylish beard, about my age or a little older.

"Yes. Do you have any more of this color?" I pointed at the can of paint. *Please don't make me say peacock blue*, I thought childishly.

He came over to stand beside me and lifted the can off the shelf. He smelled nice, like laundry soap and something spicy.

"Yeah. As long as you don't mind waiting while I mix some up. How much do you need?"

"Four cans," I said, totally clueless about paint, or how much of it I'd need to cover the whole main level of the house.

He made his way to a center counter with a big metal machine behind it. I trailed behind him.

His back was turned to me while he mixed the paint, and he carried the paint cans over one by one as he finished. He had on loose stonewashed jeans with a chain that seemed to be holding a wallet in his pocket.

A tattoo sleeve was visible, covering all—or most—of his left arm.

When he set the last can on the counter, he asked, "Are you new around here?"

His eyes were level with mine, but they seemed to be reaching deeper...

The question was innocent, but for a brief second, I caught his eyes drifting down to my chest. I suddenly felt self-conscious of my tiny breasts poking through my nearly sheer Fiona tank top.

"Yes. Well, sort of. My family owns the house

up the hill from the cemetery. Well, I own it now. But my grandmother, Doris Landry, is the original owner." I cleared my throat, hating the way my tongue was sticking to the roof of my mouth as I tried to get the words out.

What is it with boys making me so nervous? Ugh!

"Oh, cool. Yeah, I know where that is." His eyes focused on mine, instead of my chest, and he seemed to take me all in, leaving me breathless in the process. I was unsure of what to say next.

With a whisper of a smile, he started ringing me up for the paint. Just then, I realized that not only did I not get milk and bread, but I didn't even have my car. How am I going to carry all of this paint home?

My face burned with embarrassment.

I paid him for the paint, then cleared my throat again. "Um, I completely forgot that I don't have my car. I'm so used to driving everywhere and being able to haul stuff home. And my brother is bringing my car later..." My tongue was permanently stuck to the side of my cheek now. I struggled to breathe and conjure saliva, my mind frozen.

"Can I leave these here until I can come back later and pick them up?" I finally choked out the words.

The guy looked like he wanted to laugh but was struggling to hold it in.

"Sure. No problem. They'll be back here, behind the counter whenever you come back to get them. What's your name? I'll stick a note on them so my coworkers will know they're paid for."

"Dorothea," I said, wiping sweat from my brow. I spelled it slowly for him.

"I'm sorry for the trouble. Thanks again," I mumbled, unable to get away fast enough.

What a doofus! I scolded myself, making my way back outside. I still needed milk and bread, but I made a decision to pick some up from the gas station instead.

The old lady behind the counter of Sav-A-Step didn't have the same effect on me as the cute guy with the beard. I introduced myself and told her I was new in town, then thanked her for the bread and milk. I carried my purchases outside, moving toward the nearest shady spot I could find.

Leaning against the deserted church building, I pulled out my cell phone. I was happy to see three full bars as I called my mom first.

The sound of her voice brought a smile of relief to my face. "Mom! I'm sorry I didn't call last night. I hope you didn't worry. Apparently, cell service sucks at Doris's. Or my house," I corrected.

"You really need to switch to Verizon, sweetheart." I rolled my eyes, but smiled. She was always trying to get me to use the same carrier as her.

"So, how was your first night in the house?" Her voice crackled on the other end. Apparently, cell service wasn't great anywhere in this town...

Pacing back and forth, I tried to get better reception. "It was great. I slept like a dream. In fact, I barely got anything done. But now I'm planning paint colors...I can't wait for you to see it when it's done," I said breathlessly.

We talked for a few more minutes, mostly her warning me how difficult removing wall paper could be, then hung up. Next, I called Nolan. I had to ring him nearly five times before he picked up. When he did, his voice was full of sleep.

"Hey, when are you bringing my car?" No reason to beat around the bush.

Nolan yawned on the other end and said, "I'm on my way. Just give me a few minutes to get dressed, and I need to ask Cooper to follow me…"

It almost sounded like his voice was drifting off.

"Are you falling back asleep?"

"N-no! I'm on my way!" Then I heard a click. My brother had hung up in his usual fashion, without saying goodbye.

"Great," I muttered, shoving the phone back down in my pocket. Already, the milk was getting warm by my feet. Time to get back home.

Back out on the main road, I glanced both ways as I crossed. There was no traffic around—none for miles, in fact. But I did see a familiar guy leaning into the driver's window of a car, talking to a girl with bright white hair with dyed blue streaks. Her chest was so massive I could see her breasts from where I was standing.

Immediately, I realized it was the guy from the paint counter. He glanced up, scratched his beard, and squinted at the sun in my direction. If he saw me, he didn't seem to recognize me. He looked back down at the blonde bombshell, leaning against her window as his lips moved.

Feeling embarrassed about the paint all over

again, I hurried in the other direction, trekking back to my new house.

Passing the same abandoned road with the matching farmhouses, I didn't give the mysterious fence a second thought.

# ACKNOWLEDGEMENTS

Thank you to my children, for inspiring me and pushing me to my limits every day. I don't know what I would do without you.

Thank you to Limitless Publishing, for believing in me and allowing me to share my stories with the world.

Thank you to my husband, for supporting my dreams and being my first real fan.

Thank you to my street team, Flocksdale's Finest, for reading my books and being my friends. Your support means the world to me.

Thank you to all of my readers. You inspire me to keep going, and for that, I'll be forever grateful.

Thank you to Toni Rakestraw, for being the best editor a girl could ask for.

Thank you to Deranged Doctor Design for creating an incredible cover for this story.

Thank you to Lydia Harbaugh and Crystal Harms, for helping me with marketing. You guys are amazing!

Thank you to all of the amazing authors who have inspired me along the way. There are too many of you to count. But without my love of reading, there would be no writing, so I appreciate all of the other writers out there. May you keep inspiring the world, and bringing to life new writers like me.

# ABOUT THE AUTHOR

Besides my family, my greatest love in life is books. Reading them, writing them, holding them, smelling them...well, you get the idea. I've always loved to read, and some of my earliest childhood memories are me, tucked away in my room, lost in a good book. I received a five dollar allowance each week, and I always—always—spent it on books. My love affair with writing started early, but it mostly involved journaling and writing silly poems. Several years ago, I didn't have a book to read so I decided on a whim to write my own story, something I'd like to read. It turned out to be harder than I thought, but from that point on I was hooked. I'm the author of the Flocksdale Files trilogy, Horror High series, Grayson's Ridge, This Is Not About Love, 13: An Anthology of Horror and Dark Fiction, and Dark Legends: A Collection of 21 Paranormal Romance and Urban Fantasy stories. I'm a total genre-hopper. Basically, I like to write what I like to read: a little bit of everything! I reside in Floyds Knobs, Indiana with my husband, three children, and massive collection of books. I have a degree in psychology and worked as a counselor.

**Facebook:**
https://www.facebook.com/CarissaAnnLynchauthor

**Twitter:**
https://twitter.com/carissaannlynch

**Website:**
https://carissaannlynch.wordpress.com/

**Goodreads:**
https://www.goodreads.com/author/show/11204582
.Carissa_Lynch

**Newsletter:**
http://eepurl.com/chb46z